"I love this road-tripper's guide to the universe...and good bourbon."
— KEVIN FARLEY, actor and comedian

"Five friends take a profound journey hunting for a treasure of $50,000, and what they found surprised even me. *Breakfast Tea & Bourbon* is an undeniable story of celebration I welcome into my life."
— SONIA CHOQUETTE, New York Times bestselling author of *Walking Home* and *The Answer is Simple*

"At times I laughed, at times I mused. I fancied what it would be like to find the treasure. And then the story flipped, and I wondered how the heck they did it. The answer: friendship."
— JONATHAN ODELL, bestselling author of *The Healing*

"I am crazy about *Breakfast Tea & Bourbon*. It is positive, uplifting, fun, and quirky. Okay... you can have the $50,000 prize. I want Sue's gold-chained belt with the 31 rubies!"
— LISA NICHOLS, New York Times bestselling author of *Abundance Now* and featured teacher in *The Secret*

"Like fine wine, this novel satisfies. Pete Bissonette takes you on an adventure that shines light on some basic truths of life. It's a welcomed break from the craziness of the world."
— LYNNE TWIST, bestselling author of *The Soul of Money*

"Magical. Funny. Friends for life at their best."

    – CHAKA KHAN, 10-time Grammy Award winner

"I love this book! It's an amusing and upbeat story that's delightful to read. It offers an amazing opportunity to find treasure worth $50,000. That's two ways reading *Breakfast Tea & Bourbon* will make you happy for good reason!"

    – MARCI SHIMOFF, New York Times bestselling author of *Happy for No Reason* and *Chicken Soup for the Woman's Soul*

"This is a fun, wild ride of discovery and intrigue."

    – JACK CANFIELD, creator of *Chicken Soup for the Soul*, which has sold over 500 million books

"*Breakfast Tea & Bourbon* takes readers on a most unpredictable adventure into physical, philosophical, and inner worlds. It provokes contemplation, inner searching, and outward growth in an unusually fun fictional tale, crackling with humor and brilliance throughout."

    – MIKE DOOLEY, New York Times bestselling author of *Infinite Possibilities* and featured teacher in *The Secret*

"Except for maybe the pizza and barbecue, I love the way they eat. The olive spread and wild salmon recipes made my mouth water. Yes! A novel with recipes! And a $50,000 prize! What could be better."

    – JJ VIRGIN, New York Times bestselling author of *The Virgin Diet* and *Miracle Mindset*

Breakfast Tea & Bourbon

Breakfast Tea & Bourbon

a novel
(and a treasure hunt)

Pete Bissonette

⊗ Learning Strategies

ISBN-13: 978-1-935200-35-2
Library of Congress Control Number: 2016950145

"Paraliminal" is a worldwide trademark of Learning Strategies Corporation. All rights reserved. "Diamond Feng Shui" is a trademark of Marie Vyncke-Diamond.

The refurbished 1948 Flxible Clipper photograph on the cover is courtesy of Mr. Rob Roswell - "Honest Bob" of HB Industries. *You are forever missed.*

Published by:

⊗ **Learning Strategies Corporation**
Innovating ways for you to experience your potential
2000 Plymouth Road
Minnetonka, Minnesota 55305-2335 USA

24-Hour Toll-Free: 1-866-292-1861 (USA & Canada)
24-Hour: 1-605-978-2023

Mail@LearningStrategies.com
www.BreakfastTeaAndBourbon.com

for your happiness and joy

Introduction

Your Treasure Hunt

Breakfast Tea & Bourbon is first and foremost a novel to enjoy. If you are adventurous, the story can be the story of your life.

The characters in the story seek out a treasure worth $50,000, and woven within these pages are real-life clues leading to an actual treasure worth $50,000.

A physical treasure is hidden somewhere in the United States. Find it to be awarded $50,000. An additional $5,000 will be donated to the charity of your choice. The treasure hunt begins on Thursday, February 9, 2017, at 5:08 p.m. U.S. Central Time.

The treasure is hidden outdoors and is not hidden on private land. The treasure is not hidden in flower gardens, ballparks, lawns, or similar environments. You are not required to put yourself in physical peril to uncover the treasure.

Finding the treasure does not require digging with tools

of any kind. Nor does it require a metal detector. When you uncover the treasure, you will clearly know you have found the treasure because of its connection to the story. The treasure is a handcrafted object.

Leave no trace. When searching for the treasure, leave every area as you found it. There is no reason to disrupt, deface, damage, or destroy anything to find the treasure. Walk lightly. Be respectful.

The treasure is not hidden within five miles of the author's home or five miles of the Learning Strategies offices. There are no clues, documents, computer files, or anything in either location that could help you find the treasure. Everything has been thoroughly scrubbed.

To be fair, no questions about the treasure hunt will be answered by email, mail, over the telephone, or at Learning Strategies. Exceptions may be made for the media.

Clues are woven into the storyline, so first leisurely read the book and full-on enjoy the story.

Then go through the book again, searching for what could be clues. Some might be obvious for you, and others obscure. Tap into your creative and ingenious side. Just know that red herrings and dead-ends will try to slow your quest.

Stay positive and imaginative. Someone is bound to find the treasure, and that someone may as well be you.

When you find the treasure, send an email to Treasure@LearningStrategies.com. Include pictures of the front and back of the treasure for verification along with your full contact information. You will receive a response within two business days. Once verified, you will need to turn in the treasure, sign a release, and agree to participate in media interviews. You will then be awarded $50,000, and the charity of your choice will receive $5,000.

If the treasure is not turned in by August 9, 2017, as an incentive the award will be increased to $55,000.

Employees and family members of Learning Strategies and any companies involved with the production, distribution, or promotion of the book cannot participate in the treasure hunt in any way. Nor can anyone who had access to any part of the book before the official publication date.

There are surprises for you online. Please sign up here: www.BreakfastTeaAndBourbon.com. You will receive:

- A video of the author hiding the treasure in the exact spot.
- Notification when the treasure is found, verified, and turned in.
- Tips and clues and perhaps a secret or two.
- Additional chapters that may be released in the future.
- Other hunts, puzzles, and games for you to enjoy.
- Notification of interesting media events and meet-ups in local bookstores.
- Cool resources to help you live a happy and joyous life!

Have fun, play fair, and absolutely share your stories on www.facebook.com/BreakfastTeaandBourbon.

In a mythical land between the sun and the moon, the place between asleep and awake where you can still remember dreaming, lies hidden for 200 to 500 million years a magic suling adorned with jewels, tassels, and inlay of tortoise shell, hailing the triumph of courage, virtue, and wisdom, a sign that hope springs eternal, breath charms the beast, and abundance is for the taking.

1

A Booze of Contemplation

TONIGHT I RECHRISTENED MY APARTMENT "Bourbon Street." I'm hosting a bourbon-tasting party to launch our quest to find treasure. Really. I think I know where the $50,000 prize of a treasure hunt is hidden. In the morning we're off to get it, and you're coming along.

I had to slip away, because I'm an introvert who likes the idea of being an extrovert, but any such execution melts my wax. I can only pull it off by sneaking moments of me time—today on my computer writing to you, other times listening to music, sometimes letting cayenne chocolate melt in my mouth, or slipping into a five-minute meditation. I even have an easy chair in my closet so I have a place to squirrel away my sanity.

I am hearing voices in the other room and cars honking on the street below. I love this city, especially the midcentury architecture of the building across from me that can hold my gaze for hours, but those voices on my Bourbon Street are becoming a bigger draw.

Bourbon is a booze of contemplation. You can drink it while watching TV, listening to hipster cocktail music, partying, or slamming through a stack of papers from the office, but bourbon is best enjoyed by itself, when you can relish every lusty sensation that brings it life, that creates a brave new world on the tip of your tongue, the scents of your taste, a beacon to escape.

My favorite bourbon is Buffalo Trace, and that's not a clue to anything other than perhaps a mirror into my soul. I first found it in the Hermitage Hotel's interpretation of the Bourbon Sidecar. It pulled the plebeian Sidecar from the dungeons of my thinking.

Bourbons had held "no trespassing" signs for me, probably because I thought I had tasted good bourbons in other well-known brands, which apparently wasn't the case. But I tried the Bourbon Sidecar anyway, because when in Nashville, drink bourbons and go to the Grand Ole' Opry.

2 ½ ounces of Buffalo Trace
¾ ounce of Benedictine liqueur
½ ounce fresh squeezed lemon

Shake with ice, pour into a sugar-rimmed cocktail glass, garnish with a twist, and sip with your eyes closed.

Sip it in the same frame of mind as when reading a good book like this one. You're relaxed, taking time for yourself, free from distractions, feeling happy and joyous.

Bring the cold-feeling glass to your mouth, smelling the

light creamy bourbon fragrance. Let the rough edge of the sugar-rimmed glass steal your attention, sugar crystals pressing into the smiling edges of your lips, cool fluid reaching your tongue, over and under. Allow it to float. Swish it gently, taste it, swallow as you must, tongue tingling. What a fascinating flavor. Thank you God, thank you distillers, thank you ancestors of the distillers who made them possible. Breathe slowly in through your mouth, letting the sweet, complex flavors come alive. It's intoxicating before it's intoxicating. It's a meditation of presence. Can you taste lemon? the herbs of the Benedictine?

Story has it that monks developed this medicinal herbal liqueur at the Benedictine Abbey in Normandy, but truth has it that some guy named Alexandre Le Grand made up the recipe himself as well as the bottle-selling story.

That's the joy of a good Bourbon Sidecar, a ribbon scoured, a bronco bruised. Your mind can travel anywhere you want, off on fantasies, diving into words, looking for hidden treasure, or just being present in the pearl of the moment.

The party was quiet and peaceful for the first couple of hours, until the booze caught up with the contemplation. Then the word *tasting* dropped from the bourbon-tasting party. Kinda like how my mom's knitting circle transformed as sherry took hold. We cackled less, though.

Truth be told, this is more of a kick-off for our treasure adventure than a bourbon-tasting party. I found out about a treasure hunt, paid a lot of money to get a stack of clues, solved it in pretty much the first run through the clues, and now five of us will be piling into an RV to see if I am right.

Lane is our free spirit. I met him fifteen years ago first at an art fair. We found ourselves looking at the same piece of pounded-bronze, acid-etched art, which I now have in my front hall. I thought it was stunning. Two weeks later we ran into each other at a fundraiser. He was a volunteer handing out T-shirts. I recognized him instantly, and I'll tell you why later. The next week we collided manhandling broccoli at the co-op. I was getting organic and he conventional. He said, "I'm saving my organic dollars for those tomatoes. They're the best." We chatted for a bit and parted with him accepting an invite to a party I was hosting that weekend. We've been friends since.

Sue is our wild spirit laced in rubies, a little bit of a nut. About ten years before I met Lane, she and I met at a seminar a few hours out of town in the woods. We gravitated to each other believing we were the only sane people in the group. On that Saturday night a fire walk was to transform our lives. I was on the team building the fifteen-foot bed of hot oak coals. As the seminar leader took to the front of the group to demonstrate the walk, I leaned on a rake off to the side.

We were supposed to think of our massive personal goal, look up, pump our fist in the air, and walk invincibly across the coals as a metaphor for walking toward the achievement of our goal.

Only the leader didn't walk. He didn't move a muscle. He stood there for a few minutes, and then dropped his fist and walked to the side. Apparently he was not going to get any closer to his goal.

The leader's assistant took the leadership position. She thought of her massive personal goal, looked up, pumped her fist—even snorted—and didn't move. We could hear the wind blowing through the night forest. She too gave up.

I said to myself, "Ah, geez." I dropped my rake, walked to the head of the coals, thought of my goal, looked up, pumped my fist, and walked across the 1,200-degree coals. Of course,

I could have been toast, but I figured if the wilds of Borneo could do it, I certainly could. And then everyone followed me, achieving their goals for the rest of their lives. I assume.

Sue and I laughed and laughed the next morning as we walked along the river.

QB Earl is the friend we all love, but no one knows why we're friends, because he really doesn't have anything in common with any of us. Somehow or other he popped into our lives about fifteen years ago and never left. It's not that he's particularly fun, but he'll do anything. He's like rice. Not all that flavorful, but goes with everything.

Tom is an entrepreneur. I love his brains, style, sense of adventure, and steadiness. He's our balanced rock. We met when he hired me as a freelance writer to work on company marketing materials. We worked very well together and have been friends since.

Me, yes, I'm a writer. I started out working for small newspapers and then magazines and then companies, mostly as a freelancer. My newspaper days were my lentil days when all I could afford to eat were lentils. Lentils with a little brown sugar for breakfast, lentils with a dab of mustard for lunch, and lentils with mushrooms and worcestershire sauce for dinner. I'm in my bourbon days now.

By the way, my name is Nelson Ware. Friends call me Nels. Or Nelson. Never matters to me.

These guys are my family. I've often yearned for a family of my own. To watch a little undeveloped human grow. Putting up with her drawing pictures on the living room walls, comforting her after her best friend pulled her hair, helping her with schoolwork, and making sure the guy she went out with thought I was an investigative reporter who could uncover anything. That said, I absolutely have the next best thing, and I suspect we're going to have a great adventure as we go out to find this treasure together.

2

A Stack of Clues

TEN YEARS AGO I read a novel about a clandestine social club of 120 folks who met twice a year at cloistered resorts, hotels, castles, private islands, and assorted lairs. They were accomplished authors, musicians, and business people who had a deep desire to find community among bright-minded, open-hearted people. To leave all troubles and trappings of their lives behind, except for their credit cards and curiosities. To simply enjoy themselves and the mysteries of the world.

They were like a family without the dysfunction, except for the murder in Chapter Six. I would often dream about being part of the club (I am a writer, after all), and shortly I realized I was creating my own version of the club with a small group of my friends, but alas, without the murder.

A couple of months ago I was sucked right back into the fantasy when I saw an ambiguous ad in the neighborhood paper for "The League of Uncommon Gentlemen," which was coincidentally meeting two blocks away in thirty minutes. I hopped over to discover a charming, intimate hotel with a red brick and limestone facade and a gay dating club.

That's clever, I thought, and before I had time to make out what to do, I was drawn into a conversation about a more clever fundraiser and its $5,000 entry fee.

Give $5,000 and get a stack of clues to hidden treasure worth $50,000.

The charity was respectable, one of my favorites, actually, the scheme fascinating, and in the morning I was tapping my credit card number into a website to sign up. I emailed Lane, Tom, Sue, and QB Earl, and they were all in, quite eager to play with me and solve the treasure.

On the appointed day an overnight package arrived. I hadn't counted on me just looking at the stack of clues and instantaneously figuring it out. Sometimes you just know stuff. Everything had popped from the pages in the envelope into my brain, bursting out in a gasping aha!

They were disappointed I had solved the puzzle without them, but when they realized I knew the signpost to a pot of gold, they remained committed and excited. We agreed I'd guide us to the designated stops along the way to the treasure, and they'd try to solve the mystery on their own before we got there. Even though we had to take off within a week, they made arrangements to be free of work-a-day commitments so we could hunt up the treasure before someone else did.

———

It's the morning after the bourbon party, and later this morning we will head out. But now I stand in the kitchen looking at the tin of what I expected to be English Breakfast tea wondering why it said only "Breakfast Tea." Had I ordered the wrong blend? Why didn't it say "English Breakfast?"

I went to the Fortnum & Mason website to check when it dawned on me. "Dah... The tea is from England. It is Breakfast tea, and therefore English Breakfast tea." Other teas labeled "English Breakfast" were obviously not from England.

I remember the day I had my first good cup of tea as well as I imagine a chicken would remember the first time an egg plopped from her.

"Wow. What the heck is that?!"

I had drunk tea, and I had not liked tea.

Not at all.

Worse than instant coffee.

But that day the taste was as beautiful as the design of an egg is elegant.

How could tea have tasted so good? "It's good tea," was what QB Earl—Earl Snowen—said, and that led me to the Internet to do research.

Forget about all mass market teas in a bag.
Especially Lipton.
Actually, forget about any tea in a bag.
Do loose leaf tea.

Two other pearls: 1) don't steep forever, three to five minutes depending on the tea, and 2) around 190 degrees for green tea and 205 or so for black teas. Otherwise it can taste astringent and bitter.

I used to think, "I paid for this teabag. I'm going to steep it forever to suck every drool of flavor from it." No wonder I didn't like tea.

I've been heating water while writing the first part of this chapter, and I just began to steep Jasmine green, also from Fortnum & Mason.

When I first began exploring teas, I discovered I liked English Breakfast and Earl Grey blends, and I was surprised at how the taste could vary from brand to brand. I ordered up a half dozen of what folks have rated as the best blends and began round after round of blind taste tests.

Three white cups of different tea leaves sitting on a white lazy Susan. I marked the bottom of each cup, closed my eyes, and spun the lazy Susan. When the water was at temperature I added water to the cups, set the timer, waited, and sipped.

Time and time again and always the Fortnum & Mason blends were my favorite—and not just a little favorite, a lot of favorite, as if their tea man blended exclusively for me, which kinda pissed me off, because they were the most expensive when you factored in shipping from England. I signed up on their mailing list, waited for a sale, and ordered a dozen blends from them.

Now I don't try other blends, because I have a warehouse of Fortnum & Mason tea in my apartment. I can't drink it fast enough. But they are good! Breakfast and Earl Grey are still my favorite blacks (and I don't add milk!).

Soon Lane and QB Earl will be here to practice qigong with me. It's like yoga, but better. The green tea will help shake the cobwebs and keep us relaxed. It is my morning secret just as bourbon is my evening secret.

So, is my secret qigong or tea? I'll never tell.

I practice qigong nearly every day, because I feel so great when I do, especially for the couple of hours that follow. There are thousands of forms of qigong, but the one I practice is a medical form—it doesn't look medical, but it certainly looks and feels healing. "Medical" was probably a translation thing between Chinese and English, trying to give it credibility. I began practicing not long after QB Earl enlightened me to tea about ten years ago.

Qigong has to do with "qi," which is energy in the body. "Qi" rhymes with "tea." Pronounced "chee." The practice of qigong moves this energy around and throughout the body. It balances it. It breaks up blockages. And it helps the body to heal itself. It simultaneously brings me feelings of happiness and joy while keeping me healthy. It worked for QB Earl. I cannot recommend it enough, especially since I believe our purpose is to live a happy and joyous life. Some people might think their purpose is to prepare children for life, be a spokesman for wildlife issues, use humor and kindness to help people adjust to aging, grow sustainable organic food to help people have vibrant health, blah, blah, blah, but they have it all wrong, in my humble estimation. Our purpose is to live a happy and joyous life. That's it.

You may have a mission to save the world, stop people from smoking, or help distressed homeowners, and that's all fine and ducky. But happiness and joy come first. Then, in the spirit of happiness and joy, you can change the world.

Back to qigong helping QB Earl. Lane, Sue, Tom, and I laughed our way through the Wednesday afternoon at the hospital when QB Earl was having a huge malignant tumor removed from his abdomen—we weren't calling him QB Earl at the time, though. That would come later.

If you're going to spend time waiting in the hospital, those are the people to be with.

When Earl woke up, I was glad to be in the room with him, but it was tough to see a friend in the hospital, totally surrendered to the hospital, scared, I suppose, looking wiped, and feeling awfully mortal.

The body is amazing. How can we be alive? How does the body operate? Why don't I tip over when I stand on one leg? What is disease and sickness? Why did Earl get the tumor and not Lane? Or me? What is a tumor? How can something attack the body? What's the purpose? What's going on? When the body fights back, what is it protecting? What's the purpose of the body? Is it to house my mind? Is it to house my consciousness? Am I my body? Or does the body belong to me? If so, who is the me? When the body dies what happens to the me? Does *me* continue? How?

I just looked at Earl, speechless, feeling full-on love and compassion, feeling sorry, wondering why him, so thankful it wasn't me, feeling guilty for that thought, a river coursing through my mind.

The surgery was routine, Earl would make a full recovery, and he'd be free of the cancer and home on Friday. That's what they were saying; that's what we were hoping for.

We all showed up the next morning before work. I brought an oolong tea for Earl, thinking it would be a little lighter than black tea, which might be what he needed. He had a cold-looking cup of coffee on his tray.

"Look what tea they brought me," as he tossed a Lipton package to me.

I laughed. He laughed. "I had to have something," gesturing to the coffee, "and anything is better than Lipton." I gave him the oolong and dumped out his coffee. He was happy.

He didn't look much better than the night before when we had left. He looked a little worse actually. Healing takes time, I figured.

Lane brought roses. Four big imperial roses.

"That's all the money I had. Do you know how expensive these are?"

"Why didn't you get regular roses? They're ten for ten bucks."

"When you can get these? Look at them!"

They were beautiful. Probably eight dollars each. The four roses made me think of Four Roses bourbon, which tastes as good as Buffalo Trace, is a bit smoother, but almost twice as expensive. So I like Buffalo Trace. Lane probably would purchase Four Roses. No, he's smart enough to know the taste difference is not worth the money, whereas with the four red imperial roses, they were beyond gorgeous.

The four of us, perhaps the four roses, were back with Earl as soon as the five o'clock whistle blew that afternoon. I brought a cup of rose pouchong tea for him. Fragrant and delicate. I didn't bring one for me, because I knew Lane was picking up a bottle of cab, and indeed he had. He came sporting the bottle, a wine key, and four crystal wine glasses—big girl type, perfect for cabs. We toasted Earl, ourselves, and Earl being home tomorrow.

"I gotta sleep, guys. I'm not feeling well," said Earl, trying to smile, but not doing a good job of it, and leaving the rose pouchong alone.

"You okay?"

"Yah, I'm just sick to my stomach. I want to close my eyes and go unconscious. Thanks for coming by," and he closed his eyes.

We said our goodbyes to Earl, headed to the waiting room to finish our wine, and then off to a lounge down the street for happy hour.

"Alcohol doesn't solve any 'problems,' but then again neither does milk, but...technically, alcohol is a 'solution' and so is milk." performed Lane, knowing it was an old joke and not even funny.

We laughed anyway.

(Did you get it?)

"I like baths, because showers dilute my wine."

We laughed and laughed and drank and laughed.

In the morning I brought a cup of Breakfast tea for Earl (yes, from England), but his eyes were flat. Flatter than last night. I asked the nurse, but she said something about Earl needing time to recover and that I should leave. I sat with Earl for an hour or so, listening to the obnoxiously loud goings on in the hall, hearing talk shows blaring from neighboring TVs, and smelling those distinctive hospital smells. Earl slept through it all like a dog on the back porch of a busy street. At some point I left, giving his hand a little squeeze, mouthing "Heal up. See you after work."

After a day's work I stood at the nurses station. "Something's up. He was supposed to be going home, and he looks like hell. He's feeling miserable. He has a fever. What's up?"

"You're not even supposed to be here," she said. "It is not visiting hours, and you're not family."

I ignored her insipient comments. "How about a doctor? Can I talk with a doctor?"

This went on for three hours. I was in and out of Earl's room, trying to get someone's attention, only hearing, "Give him time."

Finally they wheeled him away for tests. Lane and I sat watching TV, anxiously waiting for Earl to return.

"He has severe internal inflammation from an infection. We don't know why, but we'll need to go back in to check it all." It was Friday evening, no surgeon was in the hospital, so they would have to call someone in.

At four thirty the next morning the surgeon told us to go home and get some sleep. The surgery went well and Earl was in post op. Staples from Wednesday's surgery had come loose, and waste had seeped from his intestines, causing the horrible infection.

I went back to the hospital after a few hours sleep, a good shower, and a cup of tea, but Earl was in a coma, his body fully swollen, his face looking like a fat ashen wood tick ready to explode. What had happened overnight? While they were able to close his intestine, the sepsis infection was out of control. The coma was drug-induced to give the antibiotics time to work.

The beeps of the monitors became the sands of an endless hourglass, sending me right back to the summer of 1987 when a dozen of my friends died just months, weeks, and sometimes days after being diagnosed with AIDS. I couldn't get that beeping out of my head, the hopeless fears from the past crawled on my skin, the not knowing, the questioning. Why was Earl there? Will he recover? What do I do? Who do I call? I remember Jeff lying in the bed, Barry, and Joe, Mark, Phil, and that guy whose name isn't coming to mind—ahh, Jim. Will Earl meet the same demise? Will he turn into a skin bag of bones with a dull rattle when he moves, eyes empty of the fireflies of life?

They were telling me drug-induced comas were not uncommon, we would know more in two or three days, it is possible he will be back with us by Wednesday, but there were no promises other than the sands of the hourglass kept pouring through the glass neck of our Land of Hypnagogia. But unlike back in 1987, I wasn't going to be trapped in the dream, and I headed to the Internet to learn everything I could about sepsis and comas.

In the days that followed a nurse named Caroline taught me a movement of qigong to help with my anxiety. It was so simple. There I was sitting on the flattened, not-fit-for-human-comfort sofa in the waiting room, eyes closed and hands in front of me in a prayer position separated by eight inches, feeling a strange sensation she called "The Energy." Slowly moving my hands away from each other, inhaling through my nose, and imagining energy coming in through every pore of my body as my hands reached outward. Then slowly moving my hands inward, exhaling, and sending the excess energy of stress and anxiety to the ends of the universe. I did that for twenty minutes, not by design, but because of the sheer pleasantness of the movement, a joyous feeling, an escapism not expected, but totally embraced.

I was surprised at how the memories of the 1980s softened along with the realities of the present. I hadn't ever experienced emotional stuff disintegrate in a matter of minutes before. The next day she brought me her qigong home study course, and I learned the simple exercises, healing movements that pulled me out of the fray. I was able to think clearer when at my writing desk, at the hospital, and whenever I thought of Earl and the crap he was experiencing.

Those audio recordings talked about how practicing this form of qigong can help to heal health conditions, and I began to wish that Earl could practice the exercises. Other than the stress, my health was pretty darn good, but it was Earl who needed help. Then in the last recording I learned a technique that allowed me to do qigong to help Earl heal.

It was prelude to the next level of the course that Caroline hadn't yet purchased, so I jumped online and ordered it right away, paying overnight shipping so I could learn it and use it on Earl.

The whole idea of qigong revolved around the premise that if there was something wrong with the body it was because of a blockage of that qi energy. There was either too much or not enough, like a river blocked by a dam with too much water on one side and not enough on the other. The river simply couldn't flow, and the watershed system couldn't work.

The same applied to human energy. If the energy doesn't flow, the body can't work, and disease emerges. Or so that's what the qigong master said on the recordings.

It made sense to me. It gave me cause for hope. Perhaps I could use it to help my friend through this dastardly predicament. When the course arrived I stayed up all night listening to the CDs and watching the videos and thinking I could help Earl.

The only problem I could see was figuring out where the blockages lie, but I soon found that the course taught a system of detection that made sense to me. I couldn't wait to get to the hospital to try it on Earl. Could I detect the blockages, could I bust them up, could I help bring in fresh energy, could I help Earl heal and come out of the coma?

I know how it sounds. I was a huge skeptic, but I was reaching, and I swear on my ancestors the next day I had immediate success. I felt I could detect the blockages, and I felt I could remove them. I was experiencing exactly what the course said I would, so I worked on Earl every morning for an hour, again at lunch, after work, and just before bed. I got funny looks from others at the hospital as I moved my hands around his body, but amazingly not from the hospital staff. Because of Caroline, most of them had been aware of qigong but had never actually seen someone use it diligently, day in and day out.

I could detect energy blockages by moving my hand slowly around Earl's body, about six inches away. In certain areas the feeling would change. The qigong master had said that would be a blockage. Then I would point my fingers together into a certain pose and hack away at the blockage. That would bust it up. When I felt it was gone, I'd wave it away, and then I would palm fresh energy into Earl's body. This work took patience, and it took time.

Have you ever scrubbed a frying pan that had grease baked into the surface? You scrubbed and scrubbed, and you could see improvement, but never fast enough? That was what it was like with Earl. I could detect the energy blockages and I could work to remove them, but the progress seemed so slow and imperceptible. Had I been working on a frying pan I would have given up, but since I was working on a friend, I could not give up, thanks, I guess, to the obsessive-compulsive aspect of my personality.

Ten days after beginning my mission of healing, at about ten thirty-five on a Friday night, I felt I had cleared away the blockages, but Earl looked as sickly, ready-to-pop wood-ticky, as ever. It didn't look like he was responding to what I was doing. It was somewhat disheartening, but I felt I had done what I could. The blockages were gone. Would they come back? I didn't know. Would it make a difference? I could only guess; I could only hope. I went home and fell asleep.

In the morning I got up to go to the hospital to check out Earl and his blockages and was met by the doctor. "Earl seems to have turned a corner in the last couple days," he said. "I think he will be all right. No, I know he will be all right." I could feel tingles of joy in my head as I processed what he said. Earl would be in the coma at least another two weeks, and perhaps another six weeks, but the doc clearly thought he would heal and recover.

That's the moment seven years ago I started calling Earl, QB Earl, Qigong Baby Earl. Three weeks later, they helped QB Earl wake up, and then began arduous rehabilitation. Earl had lost a lot of muscle during the Weeks of Unconscious Unpleasantness, and he needed to rebuild the muscle and learn how to walk almost all over again. But on the ninetieth day after he was pushed into the coma, he was pushed out of the doors of the hospital. Instead of bringing him home, my cohorts and I brought him to my place for seemingly endless toasts of Bourbagne, a cocktail of bourbon and champagne!

> 1 ounce of Buffalo Trace
> 1/2 ounce of vanilla syrup
> 4 ounces of Lido Bay sparkling wine (my favorite)
> Chill in a champagne glass molded from the titties of Marie Antoinette.
>
> Garnish with a vanilla bean.

Making the vanilla syrup took a little planning, because it needs to be done ahead of time. Boil three cups of water and dissolve in one cup of sugar (yes, it uses refined sugar, which I abhor, but bourbon has mysterious properties that turn sugar into vegetable, retaining the sugary taste and silky texture). Then pour it into something that won't shatter when hit with the super hot water. Scrape in the innards of two vanilla beans, stir it up, and let it set in the fridge for at least eight hours.

Perhaps the only thing better than Bourbagne is the Bourbon Sidecar, but the Bourbagne is a treat to enjoy on super special occasions, such as the return of our new semi-gimpy QB Earl!

———

Back to the task at hand, morning qigong practice and green jasmine tea. Love it!

Soon I will head out to pick up an RV for our road trip to find treasure. Yes, yes, yes, we should look within for treasure, which is what meditation and tea (or a good Bourbon Sidecar) can help with, but now our focus is gold!

I am in charge of getting an RV as our rolling base and bringing tea, QB Earl is on booze duty, Lane coffee and decorations, Sue riding food, and Tom restaurants, the trip playlist, and places to park and flush.

3

Driving the Beast

I PULLED UP CURBSIDE to Lane's apartment in a 1975 Winnebago.

"Hey, this is all we can get on a four-day notice," I said, standing in the door looking at the troops lined up on the sidewalk. Boxes and coolers, stacked neatly. "At least the sun is shining."

"Does it smell?" asked Lane.

"Probably," said Sue.

"I'll get some candles," said Lane. "Infused with Febreze."

"Infuse some insect repellent, too," added Sue. "Probably has fleas. They live in the carpet and will chew away at your feet and the first few inches of your legs. We rented an RV when I was a kid. It stunk."

Tom scanned the outside of the beast, curling his nose slightly at the crisp yellow-orange racing band along its side and a narrower red-orange band making an angular dip into the yellow-orange band, forming the Winnebago W. "It's so ugly, it's cool."

"Retro," said Sue.

"Probably gets a mile to the gallon," said QB Earl.

"It's our home! I declare it Winnie the Beast," I beamed. "Board up!"

"Winnie the Beast," laughed Sue.

"Smells like Winnie the Poo," said Lane.

"We need to purify this place with some purple," said Sue. "Tom can you play purple?"

"Give me a minute to set up the speakers," he said.

Soon the iconic, instantly recognizable opening chord of "Purple Rain" rang through the beast. Sue put down the box she was loading and, channeling her inner Prince, began a slow sway, her arms floating to the sky, hands sweeping the heavens, accepting grace, the rest of us following, me with less rhythm, gently undulating from one foot to another, one leg to the other, one hip to the other, our torsos, shoulders, and arms following the flow, time suspended, joining in the song, *I only want to see you laughing in the purple rain...purple rain, purple rain... purple rain, purple rain...purple rain, purple rain...I only want to see you bathing in the purple rain.*

Once we got out of the city, fully purpled, I thought driving the beast would be easy, but every gust of wind pushed me to the right or shoved me to the left. I clenched the wheel, fearful of tipping over, wailing as we went, thinking I was going too fast at fifty on the highway.

Then I bellowed, "SIT DOWN."

It must have sounded like a bull giving orders with clear and unspoken consequences, because everyone froze, slowly sat down, looking forward at me in distress.

Silence. The meditator had exploded. Is the world ending?

Finally the beast was tamed, becoming a gentle giant cruising down the highway. More of a Winnie than the Beast.

I had noticed through my peripheral vision that the gusts of wind pushing the beast one way or another coincided with people walking across the RV. They kept shifting the beast's center of gravity. That wasn't in the instruction manual. The beef-witted jollux that rented me the beast said nothing about passengers staying seated. But now I knew. No fast movements in the back. We'd make the eighty miles to the first stop without bruises, dents, or spilled cocktails.

QB Earl stood slowly, glancing at me to see if my brow would furl and horns would twitch, and then imperceptibly moved to the counter to mix his QB Cosmo.

Great. Cocktail time. And I had to drive. His QB Cosmo was the best in the world.

> 4 ounces of vodka (pick a different craft vodka each time and store it in the freezer)
> 2 ounces cranberry juice
> 2 ounces Cointreau
> 1 ounce of fresh squeezed lime
>
> Shake with ice. Serve with a twist of lime in a martini glass, except in an RV when a cocktail stem glass is called for (less of the martini V and more rounded to keep the goods from sloshing out).

Then the clinks followed by quietness.

"Damn this is good," someone rumbled softly.

I didn't care who. I was upfront with a slight pucker in my

mouth, tasting my memories, lost to the world behind me, eyes to the world in front.

Then Sue got up to put a pizza in the mini-oven. Oh, I love the smell of pepperoni. We're going to be fat, loaded, and rich when we're finished with this trip—assuming there would be plenty of drinking time when I'm not driving.

As Sue handled the pizza, I caught a red sparkle in the rearview mirror from one of the thirty-one rubies that adorned three gorgeous gold chains draping her hips. Me, I have no hips. If I didn't wear a belt, my pants would slide down, just like those curtains that magicians use to hide their pretty assistants. Poof! The curtains swiftly drop revealing an audience-gasping surprise. That would be me without a belt. If I were bolder I would go through life without a belt and wearing underwear patterned after a jockey's jersey at the Kentucky Derby—perhaps shiny gold with purple and green diamonds, so the audience would have something to gasp over.

QB Earl has birthing hips and pants easily cinch on him. When he walks away, you might think he was a woman unless you were to look at his head. It's a man's head, sometimes bearded. And red at that. More of a copper than soft cinnamon, or a crimson or vibrant vixen.

Sue's gold and ruby almost gypsy-like belt works on her. It's exquisite. Her eccentric great-aunt Aggie wore it all of the time, and secretly willed it to Sue. "Dear heart, dear sweet Sue, I give you the red of reds, the queen of queens. They will protect you from frightful dreams and psychic attacks, and they will bring to you an inextinguishable flame, faithful passion for life, and mystical communion. We'll meet again. Love, Aunt Aggie."

On the tenth anniversary of Aunt Aggie's death, Sue sat beneath a sprawling oak, gazing deep into the blood red cavern of one of the rubies when it began pulsating in her hands, getting so hot she threw them to the ground. When she awoke from a slumber she recalled the incident with full vividness, not knowing whether it was real or a dream. Either way, she began wearing the rubies every day. One day she had the belt appraised on the off chance it had not been a dream, and to her shock the rubies were real—$701,500 real.

Aunt Aggie and Uncle Hughie were not rich. Where did the rubies come from? None of the family knew for sure, but they all thought they were cheap glass baubles, and Sue did nothing to change their minds, only wondering whether Aunt Aggie knew. Given the letter she wrote, she had to have suspected.

Sue brings the belt to a trusted jeweler twice a year to have every link examined. Perhaps we'll examine the Mystery of the Belted Rubies in another book, or perhaps later in this one.

Aunt Aggie left Sue another gift she always wears. A hairnet of blue sapphires, which adds a dimension to Sue's appearance that simply radiates. I really love her. She's been a good friend to me for three decades. It's nice to have longevity in a friend. The gifts could not have been given to a finer person, and it helps balance the screwball nature of her relatives, including her peculiar cousin Tommy, who tried hijacking a plane to Cuba back in 1965 when he was sixteen. Nobody saw it coming. Her aunt, Aunt Aggie's niece, probably said it best, "How can you tell what happens when a perfectly normal person cracks?"

Hearing Sue tell the story, I'm not sure how perfectly normal he was, except for being a perfectly normal kid going through adolescence not knowing what to do with his growing but undeveloped brain doped up by hormones and bones lengthening as fast as our belts do as we get older. I'm surprised everyone isn't screwed up at that age. I wonder how close I was to stealing two of my dad's guns and sneaking them onboard a flight. Apparently you could do that back in the 1960s.

"He was cute, an honor student, clean cut. He even wore a suit to the hijacking, even though they lived in an end-to-end," Sue said.

"End-to-end?" asked Lane.

"Yup. It was like a double-wide, but end to end," she said.

"Gawd, that would be long. How weird. I've never seen one."

"My uncle lost his job, they lost the house, but he managed to get two mobile homes, and that's probably the best way to connect them."

"Have you ever seen a triple-end-to-end?"

Sue stared at Lane wondering just what goes on in his brain. Then she continued. "He was the smartest kid in the school, but kept to himself, reading every newspaper he came across. But we really weren't friends. We ate birthday cake together. That's about it. As news of the hijacking spread through town, all of my friends wanted to know everything about him. Even The Gray Lady wanted to talk with me."

"The Gray Lady? Wow." said QB Earl.

"What was your first reaction?" asked Lane.

"I was completely stupefied. Nothing fit. 'What? Tommy?' An airplane? He's never been on a plane. I didn't even think he knew how to shoot a gun without shooting himself. And Cuba. He wanted to go to Cuba! I didn't even know where it was other than south of Florida."

"Did he shoot anyone?" asked Lane.

"About a half hour after takeoff he got up, jabbed a pistol

in the jaw of some other passenger, walked backwards to the cockpit door waving the other pistol. He was two-fisting it. My cousin. He shot three shots into the floor, declared 'I've got a gun,' as if it wasn't obvious, 'and I'm not afraid to use it,' and shot three more shots into the floor."

"Didn't the holes in the plane cause it to lose pressure?"

"Apparently not. The guns were 22s after all, which can barely shoot through a pumpkin."

"How would you know?"

"I've shot pumpkins!" Sue exclaimed in a fit of delight, and everyone raised their cosmos to the sky cheering in unison, "I've shot pumpkins!" Even I yelled it out, trying to keep our giant beast on track when the sudden surge of people standing and thrusting their hands high caused it to roll a little.

"Hey, no sudden movements!" I bellowed back.

"Oops!" came Lane, then zeroing back to Sue, "Did he make it to Cuba?"

"No, some fearless World War II vet on the plane gave him a stiff drink, which mellowed him out. I don't think he had ever had a drink before, and probably not since."

"Bourbon?" I asked.

"As a matter of fact, it was Bourbon. Bourbon!" she cheered. "Bourbon!" cheered everyone else.

One cosmo and they were already cheering. This would be a fun weekend.

"Cheap airline bourbon?" I asked.

"Probably not," said Tom. "In those days the airlines served to impress."

"Buffalo Trace?"

"Probably Jim Beam."

"Oh," I trailed disappointedly.

"So did he pass out or what?" asked Lane. "What happened?"

"The guy who gave him the bourbon talked politics with Tommy, which was apparently why he wanted to go to Cuba."

"Not to read Hemingway?"

"Stop it. No, he wanted to call attention to the plight of Cubans—he was a Castro hater, apparently, and then right in the middle of it all someone pulled out a tube of rare gold coins as if the shiny coins could steal his attention from his militant agenda, but they did. Tommy kinda collected coins, and he'd probably much rather be home with his coins than in that plane. He was mesmerized by coins, especially those gold ones he had never seen before, and then," she spoke slowly, "he put the gun down to touch the coins."

"Ha! He did what?!"

"My Tommy." She raised her glass. "My Tommy!" everyone cheered.

"And then two guys from NASA tackled him."

"You mean NSA."

"No NASA. The astronaut people. A bunch were onboard going to a conference. *The Right Stuff!*" she cheered. Luckily no one else cheered.

"What did Tommy have to say for himself?"

"He kept blurting out stuff about the poor people suffering in Cuba."

"Did he go to jail?"

"Hijacking carried the death sentence back then, but ole Tommy was sentenced to a federal youth camp."

"What!?"

"He was certified to stand trial as an adult, but they tried him as a juvenile, and a whole different set of laws kicked in."

"What did your uncle say about him?"

"It was lame. Something like, 'He just thought, thought, and thought, and then decided with his own mind to express himself.'"

"You have his blood in you. Any thoughts lately?"

4

Persian Blues

"I HAPPEN TO KNOW that when people rent a recreational vehicle for just a few days, they do not need the awning," declared the guy who rented me an RV with an awning that didn't work.

"What? You're kidding?" I said, speaking clearly into the phone. "Drinks are poured, music is playing, the sun is beating down, and we want to use the awning."

"You don't need to use the awning."

"How will we avoid the sun?"

"Sit on the other side of the vehicle, and use the vehicle for shade."

"But we're parked on a street. We can't sit and drink cosmos in the traffic."

"I'm sorry, but you don't need it."

"If we don't need it, why did you point out the button when you gave me the tour of the RV earlier today?"

"I didn't."

"Yes, you did. You said, 'The vehicle needs to be in park. Then push and hold this button, and the awning will come down.'"

"Yes, if you use it on longer trips."

"But you didn't say that. And besides, how does the RV know we are on a shorter trip? Can you talk to it?"

"I'm sorry you are on a shorter trip, and you cannot use the awning."

I stood there completely dumbfounded. He would not fess up.

Lane and QB Earl were drinking cosmos in the sun, Sue was getting snacks ready, and Tom walked across the street to the hardware store.

I looked to the sun and toasted it, sans cheering. I love QB Cosmos.

And I toasted everyone else. I have this thing with toasting. First, you cannot drink without toasting. Then, when you toast, you must pause as you look meaningfully into the eyes of your toasting partner. I tend to open my eyes wide, allowing my eyeballs to slightly bug. That's the only way I've been able to get others to play along with me.

When I implemented the Looking Meaningfully Rule of Toasting, others didn't take to it very well. I think they didn't like that brief connection with another human, but when I bugged my eyes a little, they all played along. It's cool how everyone now really gets present with everyone else, if only for a moment. It's part of living a happy and joyous life.

Before long Tom was back banging away at the awning, and I was tasting the olive spread Sue had made back home. I had never tasted anything so good. Olive spreads are so predictable in their taste, but this was something different, something better. I gave her a big hug and toasted her and her spread, we all cheered as the awning unwound into position, and Lane hung a copper Wind Spinner of Mesmerism on the corner of the awning.

We spent the next thirty or so minutes talking about the idiots of the world who own RV rental centers, the MacGyvers of the world who can shade the sun with common tools from a hardware store, magical elixirs, and that amazing olive spread.

> 2-1/2 cups of pitted mixed olives from a deli, mixed with pepper flakes
> 2 to 6 cloves of garlic
> Almost a half cup of walnuts
> 3/4 cup of shredded parmesan cheese
> 1/2 cup of California Olive Ranch olive oil
>
> Pulse a little in a food processor, spread, and smile.

"Just what are you guys doing here," said a big-bellied officer wearing a crisp blue uniform, his eyes shaded from the sun by his visor, looking and sounding incredulous.

"Come in under the awning. Would you like a cosmo? QB Earl makes the best," said Lane who looks barely old enough to drink.

"You can't be here. This is a city sidewalk."

"Why not? Would you like a cosmo?" asked QB Earl.

"No, I wouldn't. You have to pack up and roll this elsewhere."

"Tom, I thought you said we could park here." I looked to Tom.

"We can. I asked Betty at City Hall, and she said we could

as long as we moved on by ten o'clock."

"Yes, but you can't set up shop here. You're interfering with pedestrians."

"Which pedestrians? This sidewalk is huge."

"And you can't drink in public like this."

"But those people are," said Lane, pointing to a couple sharing wine down the street.

"They are in a restaurant."

"No, they aren't. They are sitting on nice chairs on the sidewalk just as we are. Our chairs are even nicer."

"The restaurant has a license."

"Can you get us a temporary license?" Lane really was fearless. Disarmingly so. Always smiling, clean cut, and flirting. He'd flirt with women; he'd flirt with men. It didn't matter, he just flirted. And he did not let up on the officer, who I knew was in for it when I saw him make the Mistake of the Ages—looking into Lane's Persian blue eyes. It was the kind of blue you see in the lotus flower, a blue that is difficult to move your eyes away from, a blue that captures girls and boys, dogs and cats—even elephants forget what they are doing when they catch a glimpse of Lane's eyes. Perhaps that's why so many readily steal away with him for a few minutes of slippery satisfaction.

They would do things they wouldn't ordinarily do, in a broom closet just beyond the nurse's station, a hotel room sixteen stories above a conference room, or on the floor just inside the door of an apartment. It's not that he's a love radiator. He's more of an everything-is-good radiator. Those unusual blue eyes, a blue you don't see very often, somehow transform a mundane day into an extraordinary experience. It's like eating a magic beet or drinking mystical bourbon—whatever it is, it's an enchanting part of Lane that causes his friends to sometimes just pause and wonder and perhaps wish they were more like him.

"How long will you be here?" asked the officer.

"Maybe another forty-five minutes, before we go in there for dinner."

"Okay, I don't see you." He turned and walked away. "I don't see you at all. And turn down the music a bit."

I like to think we used the Law of Attraction to get him on his way, or Lane's Law of Distraction. Or perhaps my flying-around-like-angels ancestors had a talk with his ancestors who nudged him along.

I guess this is as good of a time to talk about our flying-around-like-angels ancestors. We all have them. They are the unseen helpers of life. Kinda like guardian angels and spirit guides. But different, and something we should pay attention to.

We each have more than a thousand ancestors from the past nine generations that had to come together to create us.

You see, when you do the math, our two parents each had two parents. Those four grandparents plus our two parents are six of our ancestors. Then our four grandparents each had two parents. Those eight great-grandparents plus the previous six ancestors make fourteen ancestors by the third generation. Then those eight great-grandparents had sixteen great-great-grandparents. Add them to the previous fourteen ancestors and you have thirty ancestors by the fourth generation. Follow the math, or just trust me. In just nine generations we each have 1,022 ancestors!

Over a thousand people lived lives that ultimately led to my life. One coincidental act after another. Fits of love, and probably some fits of bourbon. And that's just since the early

1800s. How many before then? And from how many counties, states, and countries? Perhaps I should do a DNA test.

The day I figured out how many ancestors I had, I gained a tremendous reverence for my ancestors and all that had to happen to get me here today.

That's one of the reasons I call on the energy of my ancestors when I meditate. That's why I'm always thanking them. I figure if I can get the souls of a thousand people who begot me sending me good energy, supporting me as my own guardian angels, then my life has got to be good. It can't be anything else but good. Even when things suck now and then, I know they are there dusting my shoulders and giving me a little goose to go forward, helping me live a happy and joyous life.

When I was a kid, before the Catholic Church fell away from me, I'd always pray to the Saints to help me with life. Saint Anthony when I lost something, Saint Christopher when my Aunt Lucy drove, Saint Thomas for school, and Saint Anne when I was sick. (It was a while before I realized Saint Anne was the saint for infertility, something I probably never needed given I was the great-great-great grandson of The Camel, whom I'll tell you about sometime.)

My neighbor, a Garrison Keillor Lutheran, once asked me why I didn't just pray to God himself. The big kahuna. That's what she did. But I explained that when I prayed to God I only got one message back over and over: You are loved. You are loved. You are loved…. It was like he couldn't hear me.

With the Saints, on the other hand, I could actually have conversations. I felt like they were helping me.

Of course, as an adult I know there is nothing better than you are loved, you are loved. That's another reason I meditate every day. You are loved. You are loved. You are loved. I sit there with my eyes closed and let God fill me with love! The saints and my ancestors are helping me with the day to day of life, but God is there for what counts most.

Anyway, that's about my 1,022 flying-around-like-angels ancestors. You have them, too, kinda like a stadium full of unseen helpers just a call away. If you believe it, they are there. If you don't believe it, they are still there, perhaps helping you find the treasure.

5

Falling Apples

THE SALMON WAS FARM RAISED, just like Lane, though he's long given up chapped udders on the prairie for a French press, cashmere, and one of QB Earl's cosmos. That mouth mush they served at the restaurant was not wild caught.

I love wild-caught salmon. Copper River sockeye is my favorite, and it is so easy to cook perfectly!

Put tinfoil on a cookie sheet in the oven and heat to 500°F.

With a super sharp knife, cut the fillet in two-inch strips, widthwise.

Drizzle on California Olive Ranch olive oil and a little cracked pepper.

When the oven is at temperature, lower to 275°F, pull out the cookie sheet, and place the salmon skin-side down.

Put back in the oven, and roast for 12 minutes.

Remove salmon from oven. If you need it to cook more, let it set on the cookie sheet for another minute or two.

Use a spatula to lift the salmon onto the plate. The skin will peel away instantly, stuck to the tin foil.

Salt a little. Toast life with wine. Eat.

Look for Copper River fresh in late spring and wine year round. We had two very drinkable bottles of Paso Robles cab for dinner. Somehow the conversation turned to religion, like wine into vinegar, a conversation that always triggers Lane, but he has a way of surviving.

Sue and QB Earl go to church regularly, Tom doesn't, I don't, and Lane walks to the other side of the street when a church comes into view. He was abused growing up, not physically, but verbally from the pulpit through a preacher who dealt with inconsistencies in life with an animosity, if not outright prejudiced hostility, for all things different. I think it would be hard for a stable church-going person not to say that Lane is one of the most Christian people on the planet, putting aside his attitudes about church.

To me it seems many in church hierarchy, from the preacher through the bishops and beyond, have no idea of the Truth of Existence. I think they learn and preach, and learn and preach, from people who learned and preached without really understanding what it is all about. I've talked with priests and ministers who don't quite get it. Yes, they are open-hearted, probably have great intentions, but I think they miss what I've discovered to be true, which is why I'd love meeting with Pope Francis. Does he know the truth? I suspect he does. Does it matter? Not really, other than as a leader of such a mass of people, it would be nice if he did.

The Lord's Prayer, in my humble way of believing, is an affirmation of truth, and it really says it all, as long as you set aside a lot of what most preachers would say. It transcends any organized religion. It doesn't belong to religion. It belongs to all of us humans. Humor me for a few minutes. I'll attempt to explain my reasoning for you without being preachy.

Our Father. I remember the day I was sitting contemplating the prayer years ago. I was thinking, if God were indeed our father, he would have to be loving. Fathers are loving (at least mine was). He could not be vengeful or mean or full of wrath as some portray God. I always knew that to be the case, because whenever I prayed to God, the message back was always you are loved, you are loved, you are loved, and the Lord's Prayer magnificently puts it in words.

I figured, since the apple doesn't fall too far from the tree, I would have to be inherently good no matter what others would say, no matter that voice in the back of my head trying to fill me with doubt, bunk, and twaddle. I kept asking myself, if I am filled with good, *who is that voice who is always criticizing me?*

That can't be me.

I would not say that about myself.

I realized that voice is not me. It's part of me, obviously, yet when it says stuff like that, it is acting more as a wart on my foot than the leader of my life.

I am better than what that little voice in the back of my head says.

Perhaps other people in society are mean and vicious because they listen to that wart of a voice. They have forgotten they are a child of God; they have forgotten they are an apple from a tree of apples.

I think if you're suffering in life, you would find a simple solution if you just sat and meditated on the idea that the apple does not fall far from the tree. Your life would be much, much, much better. That's what I believe anyway. I think Lane believes it, too, but he is looking at those apples further from the tree as villains, when in reality they are apples too, like all the others forgetting they came from the tree of apples. Spoiled apples, yet apples nonetheless.

Let's go to the next lines of the prayer.

Who art in heaven. Our father is in heaven, and we are here on the playground of earth, which is a superb place to live a happy and joyous life.

Hallowed be Thy name. If I were on the prayer-writing committee, I'd change that to "whole be thy essence." "Whole and perfect be thy essence, thy being, thy nature." That fits the God who tells us continuously you are loved, you are loved, you are loved.

Thy kingdom come, thy will be done, on earth as it is in heaven. This one is so simple for me. If as a king, God is always saying you are loved, you are loved, you are loved, his kingdom must be that of love, his will must be love, and if God is infinite and omnipresent, his love must live on earth as it lives in heaven. It cannot not!

Sit, close your eyes, think of God. Come on. Do it. Do you

not feel you are loved, you are loved, you are loved? If you do not feel it, keep sitting. Be quiet. Just sit and meditate on it. This book can wait. I think that's one of the reasons QB Earl, Sue, Tom, Lane, and I are such good friends—we know we are loved and how can we not help but love each other?

Yes, this seems sappy silly, but what a great way to live life. *Give us each day our daily bread.* As I've said, I think the purpose of life is to enjoy the playground of earth, be happy, and if you're not doing good, at least do no harm.

Our daily bread is everything essential to live on purpose, including being able to get food and all we need to sustain our lives. So yes, it is a great request: give us each day our daily bread.

Forgive us our trespasses as we forgive those who trespass against us. I've always had a problem with that line, not that I had someone I couldn't forgive, but because I believed asking for forgiveness or forgiving others involved judging. *Judge not lest you be judged.* Thank goodness I woke up from that stifling misconception. Forgiveness is one of the most freeing blessings of life.

I had two dear but miserable friends whose growing business was robbed of over two million dollars by their chief financial officer. They devoted a couple of years to recovering assets and getting the embezzler locked up. They hated the guy and loudly said they would never forgive him. I helped them anyway I could, from cleaning up assets to breaking into storage lockers and rummaging through the spoils, but I could not dissuade them of their hatred.

Everything about that story was tragic and remains so today. At some point it became clear the toxic tar coating their lives and the hate in their eyes when they talked about "the bad guy" would be with them for life, with them until death. They were the victims, damn it, and they were going to live the role and not let you forget it.

Within six years my one friend had become morbidly obese and the other was stricken with one disease after another. I see them once a year now, which is sad, but tar is sticky, and I ain't going to let it get on me.

Forgiveness. Forgiveness. Forgiveness.

The qigong master I mentioned earlier says one of the best ways to cleanse your heart and heal yourself is through forgiveness, even if you have to pretend you are forgiving.

Some people say "Forgive us our sins" instead of "Forgive us our trespasses." Same thing. We are sinners. We are trespassers.

What? We are sinners? How can the apple be a sinner when the tree of apples is not?

When we forget we came from the tree. When we forget our purpose. That is the sin. A sad sin. Our forgetting is the sin. A transgression.

Lead us not into temptation, but deliver us from evil. Perhaps there is a more positive way to put it. "Lead us through love and help us live fully as an apple from the tree." That's staying away from temptation and being free of evil. It goes back to our purpose: *enjoy the playground of earth, be happy, and if you're not doing good, at least do no harm.* Temptation lies in doing harm, whether to the expansive nature of yourself, others, or our world.

When I listened to the *Seeds of Enlightenment* recordings of spiritual mentor Jeddah Mali, I finally understood how the true nature of the universe is expansion. That we are to live a life full of light and expansion. When we go against our nature, we contract. When we do harm, we contract and exert contraction on others.

That's what we talked about as I suffered through my salmon. Yes, we are on the adventure to find treasure, but we can't forget the treasures of life that are all around us. Perfectly cooked Copper River sockeye salmon, understanding the meaning of life, one of the greatest prayers of mankind, and friends.

6

The Banishment

I'VE ALWAYS LOVED GAZING to the clouds and imagining the changing stories they seem to tell. Or driving around the country and seeing rock formations that look like animals or people, either encrusted in time or emerging into an unsuspecting world. After dinner we drove to a park, and it appeared we were driving our gentle giant directly to a sleeping giant. Would it awake and step on us? I smiled.

It's quiet now. Lane is listening to a relaxing Paraliminal with headphones—he says they help guide his nonconscious mind. The others have drifted off. We flipped coins for who would sleep where. I'm in the loft above the driving cab (where I wanted to be), Lane is on the sofa, Sue on the dinette-turned-bed, and QB Earl and Tom in the back bedroom. I got lucky on that, too, because they both are snorers of great proportion.

I hope by morning we're not smelling like sardines. We're

packed in here awfully tight. Lane brought his famous home-made candles of soy wax flakes and essential oils, and we've had one lit most of the day to purge the disinfectant smells from the RV. We paid quite a bit for this antiquated mobile motel, and it came with its own palette of smells that even pepperoni pizza couldn't mask.

We'll have to stop by a hardware store in the morning to get light bulbs. I'm sure if I called the RV rental center, the Chief of Customer Satisfaction would say, "I happen to know that at this time of year you do not need light bulbs in an RV, especially on a short trip." The five of us played Skip-Bo by candlelight before bed.

The smells of Lane brewing coffee and the whistle of the tea kettle woke us early. Lane, QB Earl, and I practiced qigong in the morning air and rising sun while Tom and Sue laced up for a run. They are the odd couple of running. Tom, tall and slender, Sue, short and...well, Sue. Tom runs with good form, Sue runs with rubies. Tom's like the wind, Sue's like a pup looking for good sniffs. Tom doesn't talk much, Sue talks nonstop.

Tom used to live in the city near us, but twelve years ago he moved out to the country to build his dream house. I know he loved the city, but I would often see him gazing at trees or up to the skies. Some sort of yearning for nature was activating in him, and he began spending more and more time with his friends Fred and Myrtle, who live just a half mile from Tom's new place, about thirty minutes out of the city.

Fred and Myrtle would be an odd couple even if they had more normal names. Myrtle, as a name, relates to love in nature. Fred pretty much means nothing, which fits because most people don't like him. I tried to like him because he was Tom's friend, and they graciously invited all of us out to their beautiful place for dinner regularly, even before Tom built his house. Everyone clearly liked Myrtle. She loved people and Fred tolerated people, much the same as we tolerated him. With respect, but without a lot of love.

For the first six years after Tom moved out there, the three of them were inseparable, sharing friends, sharing possessions, sharing ideas, sharing chores, brainstorming for each other's businesses, taste-testing booze, cooking for each other—you name it. Then Fred banished Tom from his property, and it took quite some time for them to extricate their lives from each other.

Tom needed to get his 1947 Massey-Harris 44-6 tractor and portable cement mixer from Fred's storage barn, and Fred needed to get his table saw, router table, and planer from Tom's garage. Then there was the 1,000-watt metal halide bulb and assembly for planting seeds indoors in the spring and the 1,000-watt high-pressure sodium bulb and assembly to support the little leaves. And there was kitchen stuff, garden tools, a 150-pound bronze goose fountain that Tom had given them for Christmas but Fred wanted to give back, keys to buildings, codes to gates and alarms, combinations to vaults, pallets of stone, and jugs of spiced rum. Those guys always had projects going and a good drink never too far away.

And then there were the friends. Everyone, including Fred's family, thought Fred was nuts, and the banishment could not be a normal divorce. They liked Fred because of Myrtle and Tom. Like I said, everyone tolerated Fred. Yes, he was very generous, but always on his terms and always suspicious of everyone.

There's a thick book in their story, but the three of them haven't said much about what happened, so it would be fiction with a dose of reality. Suffice it to say the banishment began one Friday evening when Tom and a neighbor were over to Myrtle and Fred's for homemade pizza.

Tom's story has never deviated one word. "Fred was being particularly negative through dinner. At one point he was calling his customers idiots, his employees dumb, and public radio a complete waste. I'm a customer of his, I like his employees, and I love public radio, so I finally said, 'Fred, you're turning into one of the most negative people on the planet.'

"'Well you know there's a solution for that,' said Fred.

"'And I've been thinking about it,' I said back." Tom never likes telling the story.

"And that's all Fred said the rest of the night except for one- or two-word answers to questions I had. I stayed another hour-plus and helped Myrtle clean up and putz. She kept telling me to apologize, but why? What did I do?" When Tom tells the story, you know he honestly didn't get what happened.

"Shortly after I got home I sent off a quick email to Fred apologizing for losing my cool, which I didn't, but what the heck. Let's have peace in the valley. Within seconds a response was back in my inbox. I knew it wasn't good, so I waited until morning to read it. I didn't want to lose any sleep over it.

"In the morning I read the email. Fred said Myrtle would be over to say goodbye for the last time.

"I forwarded a blank email back to Fred saying his email had arrived without content, and he immediately returned what he had sent before. I had given him a chance to sleep on it, and get over it, but he hadn't." Tom was miffed.

We all thought it would blow over in a month or two and they would be back in this weird threesome of a relationship again, but that was seven years ago, and alpha dog Fred kept

Myrtle on a leash, away from her best friend.

Who knows what really happened over there. Obviously tension had to have been brewing in Fred's mind for quite some time. Tom said he hadn't seen it coming. Perhaps Fred had been stewing because Tom took better care of Myrtle when she was hospitalized for cancer, or Tom's business had surpassed Fred's in revenues, profitability, and potential, or Fred crossed the obesity line while Tom stayed fit, or after six years of being single Tom finally fell in love, which upset both Fred and Myrtle.

"Good riddance!" I had told Tom. Fred's family and friends all thought Fred was a passive-aggressive backstabber. But it didn't seem to faze Tom either way. He went on with his life, buoyed by his new love, who's not with us this weekend because of an unexpected work trip (they were originally going to have the back bedroom). Tom seemed never to suffer from the banishment. Actually, no one saw him ever suffering. We friends probably suffered most. I think Tom has a great outlook on life. He knows how to put things in perspective, and not get his underwear in a bundle.

When Sue's boyfriend broke up with her, and she wanted him back, Tom asked, "Why would you want someone who doesn't want you?"

Sue kept saying how he was perfect for her, that she loved him, and on and on. Tom listened and asked, "Why would you want someone who doesn't want you?"

Sue strung on more rationalizations such as: I'm perfect for him, we travel so well, we like the same things. When she slowed a bit, Tom asked, "Why would you want someone who doesn't want you?"

Sue didn't say anything further. She looked at Tom, who

looked as sweet as ever. After about a minute of silence, Sue said, "Well, let's make popcorn," and her ex was never brought up again.

Tom is a cockeyed realist, a practical optimist, and so are Lane, QB Earl, Sue, and me. We all have our stuff, but we clearly see a half-empty bottle of bourbon and say, "Look how much more we get to drink!"

7

Continual Smelling of the Roses

Whoever first gushed "stop and smell the roses"
Had no idea of the stress she ushered onto humankind

I wake up every morning, rush, rush, rush...
to smell fresh coffee
I rush to work, rush to wrap silverware, rush...
to put out lovely fresh flowers
After work I rush to chores and rush to a bar...
to relish cocktails
I rush home to make dinner so...
I can enjoy a favorite show
Rush to clean the dishes, rush to brush and flush, rush...
to a comfy sleep

My life is rush, rush, rush...
to seek moments of magnificence

I wish I didn't know I had to stop and smell the roses
Yes those times are luscious, but I wonder whether yester-
year's mantra of simply rush
Might be better. Stress was killing you, but at least you
didn't know it.

Whoever first gushed "stop and smell the roses"
Had no idea of the stress she ushered onto humankind

Earlier this spring Lane emailed his poem to our group of friends, so I immediately convened an elderflower picnic in a park about forty minutes out of town. It was spring, and the elderflowers were in full blossom. I brought St-Germain, a French liqueur made from elderflowers, and Lane brought Italian crystal rainbow cordial glasses, which I ended up buying from Lane, because they were too pricey for his budget, but not his eyes.

"Why did you spend so much?"

"Look at them. They are exquisite. And if we are going to have an elderflower picnic, we need something to put it over the edge."

"But WE put it over the edge!"

Sue brought no-fry fried chicken, Tom made a slaw with sugar snap peas, and QB Earl brought pineapple ice cream.

We sat on a blanket on the lawn in the center of a half-moon of elderberry bushes. It was the pre-berry season. The flower season. The sun was warm, but we still needed to keep on our jackets. Sue's rubies draped below her soft denim jacket, sparkling as sparkles do. We gazed through the golden elixir in the rainbow glasses (I guess, I should say "Italian Crystal Rainbow Cordial" glasses for what I paid for them).

I declared no talking. We just enjoyed the Festival of Light we held in our hands, letting go of the stress of our lives, of the week, of what was to come, and the Festival of Fragrance and Flavors as we sipped St-Germain.

Sue started talking about elderflowers and elderberries, and I re-declared no talking, but Sue went on about birds pooping purple from the purple berries all over picnic tables in the park, how difficult it must be to clean, and how sitting on the stuff must stain, too, but soon quieting to enjoy the St-Germain, probably since everyone else was quiet, and no one engaged in her one-sided conversation. That's our Sue.

Lane writes poems now and then, and I always appreciate his perspective, how his innerness comes through in his writing, and how they often speak to the cracks in our lives. I asked him to read his roses poem as we held our rainbows. We could feel his suffering, the tugging in his life, rushing just to smell the roses.

"How come we can't smell the roses every moment?" I asked.

How can we turn our rush to work, rush to wrap silverware, rush to put out flowers into joyful moments?

How come we can't notice and enjoy the wet pavement, the beauty of the red-orange Don't Walk signs, the Movement of the People, the color and patterns of everyone's clothing, the slight palpitation when we realize we are a little behind the clock?

How come we can't enjoy the cool silver, the variations in color, the feel of the cotton napkins, the pattern of crumbs on a tabletop that someone hadn't cleaned after the last shift?

How come we can't enjoy the box of flowers that need sorting and cutting? The colors, even the absence of fragrance?

Why can't we see roses in all of our haste? Can we? Should we? Or would it just cause more stress as one more thing to do?

In that half-moon of elderberry bushes we all pledged to each other that we should not stop and smell the roses, but turn our lives into the Continual Smelling of the Roses and find the fragrance in everything we do. We didn't know if it would work, but we would give it our best.

"Cheers to the roses," said Sue raising her rainbow of elderflowers.

"Cheers to the roses," we all exclaimed.

"Okay, enough of this sweet stuff," I said, "Who would like a glass of chardonnay?! Lido Bay Seven Seas!"

It was during our elderflower picnic that we decided to take an RV trip. We didn't know when or where. The Race to the Treasure wasn't in our consciousness. It would be a while before I heard about the League of Uncommon Gentlemen. But we vowed we would take a trip, and we agreed to this prime directive: nothing gets scheduled that prevents, rushes, or forces the Continual Smelling of the Roses. In other words, no gotta-hurry-up-so-we-can... What will be, will be.

That's why Sue and Tom's morning run could stretch to two hours and Lane, QB Earl, and I wouldn't even care. We had our qigong, tea, fruit, books, morning sun, and Joe the Hummingbird, with no rushing even in our minds.

Joe? Within three hours of hanging out a bulbous, red, hand-blown glass hummingbird feeder, the first hummingbird joined our party. We named him Joe. Of course, Joe could have been a Jo, because we didn't know how to check. (But I'm sure that as soon as this book comes out, plenty of folks will point it out for us.)

8

Moms on Strike

I REMEMBER READING ON FACEBOOK, "We should start refer-
ring to 'age' as 'levels,' so when you're Level 80 it sounds more
badass than just being eighty years old." I agree.

When I was younger I always thought of old people as mo-
seying along to death. Dulled by quiet desperation, socked by
pain, slowed by memory, confused by the price of eggs, and
wearing clothes that should be burned, buried, or both.

And perhaps that described the old people I knew then,
but it certainly doesn't describe the old people I know today.
Death might be in the back of their minds, but it certainly isn't
in their sights. There's no resignation. If anything a detonation
of defiance, with places to go, great foods to eat, tea to drink,
very cool treasure books to read, and people to love. They know
they are playing at a higher level—maybe not Level 80—but
at a level that unlocks certain superpowers not even imaginable

by those living on lower levels.

Maybe Mr. Bebee of my youth enjoyed sweet tenderness with Mrs. Bebee when I wasn't around. Maybe Mr. Parker laughed himself to sleep with Johnny Carson, remembering all of the fun times he had had with Mrs. Parker, who had been long gone. Maybe Old Man Marsh enjoyed watching us play, when it appeared to me he was turning into stone.

I guess it is all perspective, but I suspect older people of today are much more engaged in their lives. And instead of feeling sorry for their impending demise, I tend to be in awe of their lives. Maybe I have more years ahead of me, but they've had wonderful years of adventures, discoveries, quests, and I'm sure, escapades, some I'll never be able to match. What lives! Not of quiet desperation, but probably of quiet exuberance.

That's how we walked through cathedrals of oaks and hickories and maples later that morning on the way to find a stone tower in the park. With quiet exuberance.

When we found the tower, it looked like it was built by people who had more muscle than imagination, more work ethic than creative expression. Along the way, while enjoying the trees of the forest, I told of the Little Apple of Death, the fruit of the Manchineel tree, perhaps the most toxic in the world. Native to Florida and the Caribbean, every part of the tree is toxic. If you were to stand under it in the rain, its milky, caustic sap would cause your skin to blister.

"How the heck do you know that?" Lane blurted out in response to that obscure and pretty much worthless fact, unless, of course, you are in Florida during a rain.

I looked to him, shrugged, and said, "Simple. I have ten more years of knowledge than you. I'm on a higher level."

At that moment I realized the beauty of getting older. I

might have less hair and creakier joints, but golly I know a lot! When I was younger I had no idea of how much I didn't know. I had no idea how empty my brain was. I had no idea the joy, comfort, confidence, and ease that knowledge could bring me. "Bring on a Bourbon Sidecar!"

QB Earl reminded me we had champagne for our hike today, which we could not drink until we found a picnic site.

"Mom didn't recognize me again last week," said Sue. We walked in silence, soaking in the beauty of the forest, letting Sue's pain breathe through us. I could not have imagined my mom not recognizing me, even in her final months. Mom was an optimist determined to get to the other side of the cancer, but the moment it was clear there would be no other side, she prepared to die. She morphed into an optimist determined for a smooth transition for her and the family. Three weeks later she breathed her final breath kissing my dad goodbye. There's probably a book in those three weeks, so watch out for what might come after this one. My heart goes out to Sue.

Tom saw a fairy house built at the base of a tree about ten paces off the path. It had pinecone pillars and a pine needle thatched roof. Little pebbles marked a winding path.

"Is she happy?" asked Lane.

"Yes, always smiling. Remembering stories from the way past. Singing spontaneously, and totally oblivious to the recent past," said Sue. "It's as if she doesn't know. As if she doesn't remember what it was like to remember."

She laughed, "You know, it is so surreal. I came into her room, and she looked frightened by my presence."

"I guess I would be too if a stranger came into my room," said Lane.

"Exactly," said Sue. "I took a breath and said, 'Hi mom. I'm your daughter, Sue.'"

"'Oh, my daughter. I must know you then,' she said. 'Yes, mom,' I said back to her. 'And you love me so much.' And then she said, 'Oh, I must. You are so beautiful. Come here and let me hug you.'" Sue smiled, with tears dripping from the corners of her eyes.

"I'm sorry, sweetie." I hugged her. A blue sapphire caught a ray of light filtering through the trees.

"That's so much better than other stories I've heard. I have a friend whose mother would curse up a storm saying words she had never uttered before in her life," said Lane. "She became very mean and vicious."

"Well, we have something to celebrate then," said QB Earl. "Sue's mom happily rolling through another phase of life. Let's open the champagne."

No resistance from any of us, we sat down by the fairy house, and with the champagne flowed stories of our moms.

"I was sitting on a kitchen chair crying, because I fell and scraped my knee on the sidewalk. It was bleeding. I was whining. Mom was making dinner. She picked up the butcher knife and walked toward me intending to cut the roast. I screamed, 'No, don't cut it off, Mom, don't cut it off!'"

That was me. When I was six.

Tom told how he came home from school one afternoon, ate the cookies his mom had set out for him, and whined and whined about something. His mother was washing the windows and in frustration threw the bucket of dirty water at him.

Sue told how when she went off to college her mom went on strike. Things had to change. She refused to continue the cooking, hauling laundry down to the basement, washing everything, and putting it away, all by herself, day in and day out. Sue's dad and her brother just laughed. But her mom got her girlfriends to picket the house and call the local newspaper. The next day "Moms on Strike" made the front page and changes happened in houses up and down the street. "A lot of guys on the street blamed my dad," she said.

"When my parents dropped me off for my first day at college, they drove away in the station wagon, Mom yelling out of the window, 'Remember, whites in hot, colors in cold, and everything else in warm!'" said QB Earl. "Every other kid around looked at me in horror, so grateful it wasn't their mother."

"And probably taking notes about the laundry tips," laughed Sue.

With the champagne bottle empty, we made it back to the path and wound our way to the misbuilt tower. None of us were inspired to climb the uninspired tower, but we imagined the view to be super, so up we went. And then down we went, walking through the woods to a gorgeous quarry we had seen up above. A perfect place for the picnic.

We heard someone playing a flute, softly echoing off the traprock of the quarry as we walked toward it. We kept on walking because someone was filming the young flutist, probably in her late 20s, and we didn't want to interrupt. We stopped in a grove of trees, still able to enjoy the enchanting music. QB Earl popped our last bottle of champagne, and Sue unpacked the last of the homemade lunches she had prepared in advance. From now on it would be restaurants.

QB Earl vowed never to haul heavy bottles of champagne around in a backpack of ice again. Lane, with his last half flute of champagne, walked over to listen to the other flute, sitting on an outcropping of rock, me wondering if I should warn her about his Persian blue eyes.

Lane caught up with us on our walk out, bubbling about being filmed for an interview about the flutist and her unusual bamboo flute adorned with beads of glass and stone.

"The filmer asked me about the experience of listening to her in the quarry. I didn't know what the film was about, so I just babbled. They were probably some friends making something for YouTube." He turned to Sue, "Run over and catch them. You love to babble. They might get something useful from you."

"Really?" asked Sue. "Are you joking? Would they want to hear me? Of course, I would talk about the joy a flute can bring to people." She darted off.

Better them than me, I thought, not one for attention outside of my tribe, which of course doesn't reconcile with me writing a book, but life is full of paradoxes.

Doing this treasure hunt as a group was a great idea. We really didn't need to have the hunt to rent an RV and go on an adventure, but what the heck. It worked.

I was not 100 percent sure we would actually find the treasure. I thought so, but I was absolutely sure the others were enjoying the hunt. Each had a set of the clues to study and unravel, but I would not tell them my solution, or even where we were heading. As far as they knew the treasure could have been in the quarry.

They've been putting their heads together on and off these past two days, googling this, googling that, putting in more time than I did to solve it originally. And whenever I would come close to them, they would change the subject, cover their phone screen, or say something like, "Hey, let us try to figure it out on our own."

9

My Froggy is Named Nelson

I GOT A GIRL PREGNANT THE FIRST TIME I HAD SEX.

What are the chances? One hundred percent. My great great great grandfather was Hinds, The Camel, a prodigious reproducer, I hear. And let me tell you about the first time I made coleslaw.

The recipe called for six cups of shredded cabbage and one cup of mayonnaise. I used six cups of mayonnaise. That's just in my nature.

Why then didn't she bear twins or triplets? The rest of the eggs drowned, I suppose.

Still, I didn't want the kid and I didn't want her. It seems so unenlightened, I know, but I was there for that fifteen-second experience. All I remember was the very first sensation and thinking, oh, my gawd.

She didn't want me, either, and she didn't want the kid, a

relief for me. Her mom arranged for adoption, made me write out a check for sixteen hundred dollars to cover medical expenses (which was down to the second from the last dollar I had in my savings account, the minimum the bank would allow me to have without closing the account—she had some compassion), and forbid me from ever seeing Valerie again and certainly not be anywhere around during the birth. Heck, I could barely remember what Valerie looked like. I remember the party where we met. A friend had just dropped out of auto mechanic tech school and wanted to celebrate not following in his father's steps. He had no other plan, but he didn't care. He just knew he wanted nothing to do with wrenches and pickle forks, the tools of his father. Everyone brought beer, Mountain Dew, rum, Southern Comfort, you name it.

I drank only to drink. It was long before I had discovered the difference between bum booze and good booze. I had been telling my younger nephews that alcohol was poison, something I had to redefine as we got older. Bum booze is poison. Good booze is divine. Today I drink because I love the flavors. The buzz helps, too. But then it was about—hey, I don't know what it was about. I didn't like the tastes, I didn't like getting drunk, I didn't like the next mornings. Maybe it was all social. My friends did it and so did I. And I'm sure it helped me out of my shell.

Valerie worked hard that night to pry open the shell. Typically the guy would have been the one looking for the oyster, but her hands were all over me. Before long we were on the couch-that-needs-replacing in her girlfriend's apartment for my fifteen seconds of fame.

I thought of the kid nonstop for the next eight months after I found out Valerie was pregnant. And for several years after that, praying that the kid got off to a wonderful life with its adoptive parents, wondering whether it was a boy or a girl, whether it looked like me.

During this time I struggled personally and got a part-time job at a car wash to pay off my credit card. My assignment was to wipe off water drops when cars emerged from the scrubbing tunnel. I was faster and more efficient than any other kid there. I could size up a car, map out the wiping plan, and dive in with towels in both hands, wiping and whirling like a somewhat controlled Tasmanian devil. I had to keep my mind going to stave off the job's inherent tedium.

I was wiping down a red-orange Camaro one morning, with my left hand working on the passenger window and right hand on the windshield, and my eyes watching a cute girl with red curls playing with a fluffy, big fat frog, wearing a gold crown, a Frog Prince. We smiled at each other as I moved to the hood and then the other half of the windshield, slipping into slow motion gazing into the hazel eyes of her mother, pausing the wiping and my breathing. It was Valerie.

She rolled down the window.

"Hello, Nels," she said.

"Hi," I said slowly, not knowing what to say.

"I'd like you to meet my daughter, Judy." She pointed to the little girl and said, "Judy, this is an old friend, Nelson."

"Hi, good to meet you. My froggy is named Nelson, too!"

"It's good to meet you, Judy. You have a handsome froggy and beautiful curls."

"Thank you." She resumed playing with her frog, telling it, "That man over there is named Nelson, too. He thinks you're handsome. Isn't that nice!" She looked at the frog as if it were saying something. Then, "Yes, that's right." And she laughed, continuing the conversation with her frog.

I looked back to Valerie.

"I just couldn't let her go," she said.

I so much wanted Judy in my life. "Could I…"

She interrupted me. "No."

"Are you…"

"No, I'm not married."

"Where are…"

"I'm still at the clinic," she said. I'm not sure whether she actually finished my sentences or whether it is my romanticized remembrance.

"We should go. It was nice to see you."

She started rolling up the window. I said, "Let me finish wiping your car."

"That would be nice."

As I finished the wheels, I banged gently on the trunk, and she drove away. Judy waved at me as they turned the corner, holding my eyes.

―――

It would be about a hundred miles to dinner. Tom found an old dining car restaurant. We all figured the food would be horrible and they wouldn't serve cocktails, but we figured we could have happy hour in the parking lot and suffer through any bad food.

Sue was riding up front with me, reading one of the *Fletch* mysteries she picked up for fifty cents at a used book store. She loves Chevy Chase, remembered the *Fletch Lives* movie, and thought she'd give the novel a try.

"Mysteries often hide a big clue for me and my life," she

said.

"I didn't know you liked mysteries."

"Well, I really don't. At least not any more than any other type of novel. But for fifty cents, and a clue to my life, hey, why not?!" She smiled. And I'm sure if she held a QB Cosmo, she'd be raising the glass, but instead I heard more about the story.

QB Earl and Tom were napping in the back and Lane was listening to a Paraliminal. He has a secret big goal and has been listening to those sessions to help out. He won't tell us the goal. I think he should, because he knows we would be supportive, but he is afraid of jinxing it. I think he is going for the restaurant manager's job.

Lane has been using Paraliminal recordings for a while now. People use them to resolve emotional issues and help achieve goals. Lane has been listening to one called *Belief* to help shore up his belief in himself.

I like them, and I know they've helped me be a better writer. You should try one. Actually, everyone should. I'll set one up for you to try free on my author's website. Plan on listening with headphones, because you will hear a voice in each ear speaking to different parts of the brain. It's pretty cool.

Lane bought the entire collection of nearly fifty different programs—you can use them for most any change. I pray to God Lane doesn't listen to the *Instantaneous Personal Magnetism* program, he's already more magnetic than any human should be. (Maybe that's the one I'll arrange free for you!)

"What are you smiling about?" Sue asked, closing the book.

"Nothing. I was just thinking of what might happen if Lane ever used the *Instantaneous Personal Magnetism* Paraliminal."

She yelped, slipping to giggles. "God help us!"

"Say," she said, "I've been using the *Anxiety-Free.*"

"You? What are you anxious about?" I asked.

"Not much. It's just that I worry a little too much about what others think about me."

"You? You're kidding. You're fearless."

"No, I'm not. I really have to work at it."

"Has it worked for you?"

"I think so. It seems to have filed burrs off my life. Last week a cabbie was driving too aggressively for my taste, so I asked him to let up a little. I never would have done that before. I would have been too scared of what he would say. But it just flowed out."

She turned back to reading her book, and then out of the blue asked, "Are you still setting money aside for Judy?"

How did she know I had been thinking of Judy? Maybe those rubies were activating.

It had been twenty-five years since I saw Judy and froggy at the car wash. Within a couple of months I had turned the corner financially and started sending five hundred a month to Valerie at the clinic. I'd write "for Judy" on the memo line of the check.

That first month I eagerly tore open the envelope from the bank to see if Valerie had cashed the check, and she had. She had written across the top of the check in red, "Thank you!"

Month after month, year after year, I'd get that little touch-in with my daughter. At Christmas I would send an extra fifty dollars with a note, "Can we get together sometime soon?" Never anything but a "Thank you!" back, usually in red, but sometimes blue or purple. I'm not sure she ever wrote back in black ink.

Seven years later I got a call from Valerie. "Everything all right?" I asked.

"Yes, very much." Judy was in fifth grade, an A student, master of the jump rope, babysat for the neighbors, wrote in a secret diary, played in the elementary school band, and kept froggy on the top shelf in her room.

She said my monthly checks always came at the right time, because she barely made enough to pay the bills without asking her mother for support. My checks kept her mother away.

"Every Christmas I would buy Judy presents and mark them from Santa."

"I guess it is better than marking them from The Sperm Donor."

"Nelson, come on. Judy knows you as my friend. I just didn't think it was appropriate for you to send gifts when we don't see you, so I signed them Santa."

"I wanted to come and visit. Even as your friend."

"I always made sure she got something fun from you and not just socks and underwear. Her favorite was a princess tiara. When she opened that present, she gasped, and ran to get froggy. 'We both are royalty now!'"

"I hope you are calling today so we can get together. I'd love to see you and Judy."

I could hear static on the phone line as I stood there waiting for Valerie to speak.

"I'm getting married, Nelson."

It took a few seconds, but I managed to say, "Wow. Congratulations. I am really happy for you. Does Judy like him?"

"She loves him. Absolutely adores him." Her voice trailed into more static, as if a big *but* was coming.

"He wants to adopt her, he wants you to sign all parenting rights to him, he wants you to agree never to try to contact her or me again, and in return he would like you to keep your monthly payments and spend it on your own life." She spoke quickly, as if she were reading from a script.

The static was deafening.

"But," I drawled, "I have already signed away my rights. Your mother made me sign all of these documents, and she made it clear I needed to stay away forever."

"I'm sorry, Nelson. I didn't know anything about that until last month. She never told me. I just thought you were being a jerk by staying away. None of what you signed was binding. It was just mother forcing you away from me and Judy. I wanted to call you from the hospital, and my mother said she would."

"But, she…"

"I know. And in the months to come she'd call you a hateful string of names, convincing me you wanted absolutely nothing to do with me after I decided to keep Judy."

I couldn't say anything. My mind was blank. No words. No pictures. No feelings. Just, "This does not compute."

"When I saw you at the car wash," she broke the silence, "and I could feel the love you had for Judy, even though it seemed you were having a lousy life, at your core was pure love, and I was so happy that you were part of Judy."

At this point I was crying. "But since you now know, why push me away? Let your long-lost friend come into your life. I'll keep the secret."

"Because Frank isn't letting go of mother's story, and after all of these years, I finally have someone who loves me, and I don't want to make this a battle issue."

When we hung up the phone, I fell to my knees, heaving dry sobs. Finally resting my head on the floor, looking up to God, I implored, "How can the kid I didn't even want have such a tug on me? What do I do?"

Within two weeks I was signing the papers she wanted, Frank wanted, her mother wanted, but if Judy knew, I'm sure she would not want. But I signed. I can't say I regretted the decision, but it has been on my mind every day since.

No, it hasn't.

It's been in my heart.

At first, haunting my heart, but after a year or so the haunting transformed into a feeling of pure love for Judy. After signing the papers, I no longer sent checks to Valerie. Instead I opened a college account for Judy. When I never heard from her around college time, I changed it to a down payment account for her first home. When she turned 21 I tried finding her, but someone told me that Valerie and Frank divorced some years earlier, and Valerie and Judy moved from town.

So I told Sue, "Yes, I'm still putting aside money for her. The fund is just over two hundred thousand dollars."

A big tear rolled from my eyes, Sue leaned over and kissed my cheek. And then Lane slobbered a wet one on my cheek.

"Hey, I don't know what's going on up here, but I opened my eyes after finishing the Paraliminal, saw all of the love, and figured I'd join the party. You okay?"

"Yup."

A few minutes later I told Lane, "Please wake up Tom. We are getting close to town. Time to direct us to the diner car. And QB Earl needs to get a shaking."

10

Batwing, Bowtie, and Butterfly Inversions

YEARS AGO I SAW "BODY SLAMMIN'" professional wrestling in some small town, a traveling carnie of sorts, where the guy who unloaded the ring from the truck also sold tickets and was the ring announcer.

The wrestlers arrived in two RVs. A newer one for the good guys and a hobbler for the bad guys, not even as good as our beast. We ran into the troupe at a restaurant where the bad guys sat in the smoking section banging their silverware for service. The good guys sat in the nonsmoking section, relatively well mannered.

That had to have been part of their barking scheme, because it got us to go to the event.

In the opening match Boris grunted around the ring carrying a Soviet flag when the ticket-taker-turned-announcer introduced him. The crowd booed. Someone threw a beet into the ring. I halfway expected garbage flying from the stands, but it was the lone, mushy beet, hurled without backup. Boris stomped on it, red oozing, the only blood-like substance we'd see that night.

A muscled pretty boy climbed into the ring to cheers of the crowd. Boris launched the flag into the stands, snorting, attacking the pretty boy. The announcer dove under the ropes. Within seconds Boris stood in the middle of the ring spinning in circles while holding onto the arms of pretty boy, who was like a moon uncontrollably pulled under Boris's spell, centrifugal force coaxing pretty boy to sail off into the universe. Then Boris let go. The pretty boy flew square into the turnbuckles of a corner and...crash...the ring collapsed. Apparently the ticket-taker-turned-announcer hadn't tightened one of the nuts under the ring.

It took almost an hour to rebuild the ring, but the 3.2 beer and pretzels helped the time fly. As we walked out later that night, we saw girls gathered around the door of the bad guys' RV, like flies to the light. Or, perhaps in this case, garbage pile.

Anyway, the bad guys were doing something right. Their RV was rocking, creaking, rocking, and the good guys' was silent. Apparently it was all part of the show. The bad guys got the girls.

———

If you had walked past our RV parked outside of the dining car restaurant you would have smiled thinking the rockin' meant a lot of wild and crazy sex, and you would have been wrong. World War III had broken out inside and we were at each other's throats.

QB Earl received a text from his brother who financed a new Mercedes, knowing full well his brother was already in hock through the rafters of his oversized house and the ball joints of his car, if indeed cars still have them.

He threw his phone at the sofa, yelling one hairy big bad word after another. "Knock it off," said Tom with an intensity I hadn't heard before.

"Never mind," said QB Earl, spinning toward Tom, forcing glare into Tom's eyes.

Tom softened and turned away. QB Earl reached out, pulling Tom's shoulder, "Don't you turn from me."

Tom turned with QB Earl's tug, returning the glare, probably holding his breath, tensing his muscles.

"Hey, calm down," said Sue, stepping to QB Earl. His arm came out, pushing her back.

"Just leave me alone," he cried full throttled, yelling about his brother, kicking a box, and throwing a pillow onto the counter, knocking over glasses and booze bottles.

With staccato strength, Tom averred, "Earl Snowen stop it. Stop it."

It didn't get through. QB Earl continued ranting, flailing, smashing, contracting. The kid was out of control.

The botched surgery was certainly life-transforming for QB Earl. Although you couldn't tell it now, he became more optimistic, forgiving of others, open to the great possibilities of life, and immensely thankful for all of his blessings. But he had this dark side that could suck a nut from beneath a wrestling ring, collapse everything around him, and unleash this turbulence in the belly of our beast.

In a fit of sanity Sue ordered Lane to get headphones on QB Earl and crank up a Paraliminal. That thought alone lifted Lane out of his dazed stupefaction. He grabbed the headphones, grabbed QB Earl by the shoulders, and forced him to look into his eyes. "Listen." Lane put the headphones on QB Earl, who immediately calmed down. QB Earl slowly mouthed, "I'm trying my best." Now, who knows whether it was the Paraliminal or Lane's Persian blues, but the RV quit rocking.

We all settled down, hearts pounding, saying nothing, just sitting, and finishing our QB Cosmos. Sue went out for a walk. I still had tension in my shoulders, my blood pressure was up. It was nice to have mellow, and it was time to practice forgiveness.

QB Earl—especially since his Coma of Great Inconvenience—and the rest of us subscribe to Auntie Mame's not-famous-enough advice, "Live! Life's a banquet and most poor suckers are starving to death!" Yet Earl clearly is in the camp that the absence of debt trumps extravagance for peace of mind, a camp his brother hasn't found.

As we all saw, and if I may make an exceedingly obvious understatement, the creation of debt saps QB Earl's peace— even when it is not his debt. It tips his emotional teeter-totter and triggers unpleasantness in others. But like a good roller coaster with full-on batwing, bowtie, and butterfly inversions, it all comes to a graceful end, although stomachs may churn for a bit thereafter.

The funny thing was, the instant he threw his phone across the RV, I knew his inner beast had awakened, and I'm sure all Lane could think about was the expensive phone and the notes to the treasure hunt. I guess Maslow's Hierarchy was on display.

We all ardently believe—or at least want to believe—that we are magnificent spiritual beings having a go at it here on earth, and when we stub our toes to trip up someone else, it doesn't mean we are any less magnificent, although we sometimes forget it and get dragged into a row. But, as I mentioned earlier, the QB Cosmos helped.

Sue came back from her walk a bit energized, waving a set of copper dowsing rods in the air. "Nels, get this buggy moving before QB's Paraliminal is done. We're sitting on a negative energy vortex, and it is a doozer."

I jumped into the driver's seat, yelling out "Hold on!"

"Let's go to Big Bob's Bar-B-Que," said Tom. "We'll come back here for breakfast."

11

It Leads You to the Golden Ring

SUE HAD ORDERED A COURSE called *Diamond Dowsing* from Learning Strategies, the same company I got the qigong course from and Lane the Paraliminals. I guess we all found their website fascinating. Coming back from her walk with the dowsing rods, though, was the first time I had any indication Sue took the course seriously.

Apparently, she drove those dowsing rods expertly, tuned into the vexatious energy vortex, and got us out of there. I suppose the key to using tools like that is not to test to see *if* they work but *how* they work.

I wish I could figure out how Tom's mind works. Why would he want us to head to a barbecue joint? He had his fill of smoked food during the Fred and Myrtle days. They smoked meat almost every meal. They even smoked pizzas. That overly smoked taste got pretty old for all of us, and it was probably carcinogenic, which undoubtedly accelerated Myrtle's cancer. But, Tom wanted Big Bob's.

Big Bob's was in a one-story, 1960s-style concrete ware-house with worn striped awnings. A big meat cooker chugged like a locomotive along one end of the building with hardwood, nutwood, and fruitwood, reminding me of Walt Whitman's "madly-whistled laughter, echoing, rumbling like an earth-quake," rousing my saliva glands, puckering my tongue. I had to get in there, and fast. Me, an almost vegetarian, drooling for meat? Smoked meat, at that? What was happening?

The parking lot was full and not so friendly to our beast. A big television station van took up a lot of space. Maybe they were filming Big Bob's madly-whistled laughter action.

We stood at the bar waiting for a table to open, me with a robust, coffee-infused vanilla porter. Dark and thick. I'd prefer bourbon or wine, but the only bourbon they had looked as cheap as I imagined their wine to be. Craft beer from the tap seemed to be my best option, and it was creamy good.

We sent Lane on a reconnaissance mission to check out the commotion in the corner. Some gal was strumming and sing-ing. Sounded pretty good to me, but it wasn't the "Great Balls of Fire" I was halfway expecting.

Lane came back just as our table was ready, and he was beaming.

"It's the Quarry Girl!"

"Quarry Girl?" asked Tom.

"Yes, the same girl from the quarry—the girl with the flute. The cameraman interviewed me again and so did the TV sta-tion. They're doing a story on this woman."

"You're kidding," said Tom.

"Whatever," said QB Earl, passing out menus.

"No really. The TV station is here doing a story on her."

"Why her?" I asked.

"Apparently more and more musicians are just showing up in bars and restaurants without a paid gig. They just set up, play, collect tips, and sell CDs."

"I heard about that," said Sue. "Sometimes they get booted out, and other times the manager loves it along with the rest of the folks. That's how my cousin Karen began getting gigs. She and her band just showed up and made some money in tips, but soon they were telling other bars about the places they were playing, leaving out the important piece about just showing up, but it was enough for bars to begin paying them."

"I suppose it would be good if the music fit with the place," Tom said.

"Exactly," I said.

"You should be interviewed Nels," said Sue.

"Why in God's name me?"

"I don't know. You brought us here. You saw her at the quarry. It would be a nice twist to their story," said Sue.

"No, I'll pass," I said.

"What are the odds of seeing her here?" asked Sue.

"Ask your rubies." Lane beamed.

Sue rolled her eyes. She often jokes that the rubies opened a portal to great intuition and psychic ability, and Lane was just playing to her. Me, I really don't think she is joking other than deflecting attention. I think wearing the rubies did help release a gift, as they did for Aunt Aggie. She knows it, too, but doesn't admit it.

"Come on, Sue. Ask your rubies," I nudged. Lane bounced in anticipation.

"All right," said Sue. "I am kinda feeling that buzz I get."

"Beer buzz?" asked QB Earl.

"No. I get to feeling a buzz up here." She rubbed her forehead. "And it is buzzing."

"And?" I asked.

She closed her eyes. We watched intently, oblivious to the music and noise.

"I keep seeing that guitar and flute girl. I think we will run into her again."

"Ha! Fat chance," said QB Earl.

"Ready to order?" asked Tom.

"Was it real?" I asked Sue.

She looked at me quietly. "Yes. I think it is real. I think we will run into her again."

"We'll find out!" I said, raising my glass.

"We'll find out!" everyone said in unison clinking our glasses together, looking meaningfully into each other's eyes.

That's when I saw in the light above the table how dirty the glasses were. Damn, I thought, I should have ordered bottled beer.

I ordered myself some baby back ribs, baked beans, and slaw. Another beer. Two stacks of napkins—one for me, and one for the bathroom. They were out of paper towels, and I wanted to make sure the cooks could wash their hands.

We were jabbering away when platters of meat arrived along with a crock of beans, bowl of slaw, cornbread, and green beans. The menu hadn't said anything about family style, which was fine by me. The waitress said, "We just kinda mix it all together and let you all fend for yourselves. Anything else, honey?"

We all dug in, and soon I had sauce up and down my face when suddenly lights shined on me and a reporter shoved a microphone to my mouth.

"Tell us about your experience running into our musician in the quarry," said the reporter.

I rolled my eyes, took a breath, smiled and said, "My friends and I were hiking through a park and heard beautifully enchanting music echoing from a rock quarry. As we walked closer we saw her, and it was... actually, I don't know what to call it other than beautifully enchanting. Almost other worldly. And now we run into her playing the guitar. What are the chances?" I smiled and went on to eating my ribs. He kept filming for a couple of minutes, I assume to get some B-roll or something.

About a half hour later a guy stopped by our table and asked how it all was. I asked, "Are you Big Bob?"

"Why? Because I am fat, covered with meat grease and barbecue sauce, and smell like smoke?"

I couldn't tell whether he was joking, ornery, or a jerk who likes to cook and should never meet his customers. I looked into his eyes. "Yes."

"Well I am." And he let rip a laugh as loud as his cooker is big and smokey.

Everyone told him how much we loved the food—it really was superb, even the green beans were not overcooked as they so often are in dive places. They seemed fresh, not canned. The baked beans made from scratch, with a unique flavor twist, not canned. The cornbread, mixed there, not from a box, with fresh jalapenos, grated cheddar, and corn. And how fortunate Big Bob was to get the publicity of the TV station. What fun! Lane shot a group selfie including Big Bob, we ordered another round of beer, and Tom wondered how to tell Big Bob to tidy up the place.

When it came time to settle up, Lane was all over all of us

to make sure we tipped well. For years I've been a solid 20 percent tipper, but Lane pushes us up. He, Tom, and I were out to dinner some years past when Lane was promoting a higher tip. Tom pushed back. "That's a lot of money," he said.

"The waiter earns minimum wage," Lane said. "We have to help him with a decent living wage."

"We aren't responsible for his wages," said Tom. "The restaurant pays him, and we tip him to express our gratefulness for his service."

"They don't pay him enough."

"Is that our fault? He chose to work here. He knew what the wages were."

"It doesn't make it right," said Lane.

"Magnanimous," I said.

They looked to me. Tom's eyes furled a little. Lane's mouth opened.

"Altruistic," I said.

"What are you saying?" asked Lane.

"I'm saying so what. So what if the restaurant underpays their employees. Who cares about the reason, whether they simply can't pay more or the owners want more profits. We can choose to be kind and considerate and give a healthy tip. Besides, we can afford it. It will make their day."

"Right on."

"I can agree with that, but even for lousy service?" asked Tom.

"Absolutely," I said. "Maybe they are short-staffed, maybe that guy sitting at the table in the corner is a jerk, maybe the waiter was up all night with his kid, so what. We can help him rise above his circumstances. We can help him be happy."

"That's right," said Lane, almost smugly, but not too much,

being grateful for my support, I'm sure.

"What if he is just plain a lousy waiter?"

"In our world, he is a great waiter having a lousy day. We are adults. We can put whatever meaning we want to onto his actions. Let's go for meaning that will make us feel better. Besides, it is better to be forgiving and generous than sanctimonious."

"That's right," said Lane. "Whatever that means."

A waiter will always overtip, even though they can afford it the least, like Lane. They know the life of the waiter and tip in solidarity, comrades in arms.

A couple of years ago I asked Lane if I could throw him a birthday party. He lit up. He always loves a party. Sometime later he said he appreciated the gesture and asked if I would get him the *Spiritual Codes* home study course instead. That's another Learning Strategies course with Marie Diamond, a Feng Shui master and creator of the dowsing course Sue had. Marie was one of the stars of the hit movie and book, *The Secret*. Like attracts like, you are what you believe, and so on. I ordered Marie's home study on Feng Shui and Lane snatched it from me before I could listen to the first CD. By that weekend he was moving my furniture around and telling me to keep the toilet seat down so prosperity didn't flush out of the house. He made sure I knew I needed to sit at the head of the table at my dinner parties, and he tried to get me to turn my desk away from looking out of the window, instead aimed toward the door.

"But I love looking out the window when I write. It inspires me. It relaxes me," I said.

"But," said Lane in a bigger *but*, "you want to be facing the flow of energy coming into your room so you can answer the call of the universe. Looking out the windows puts your back to the benevolent universe."

I gave in to his insistencies, because it did make sense, and turned the desk in my den to facing the door, and I began getting more freelance writing gigs almost immediately. So, when Lane asked for *Spiritual Codes*, I was quite okay with getting it for him, knowing he would study it and come back to me with suggestions for something or other.

"I've been waiting for you to order the course," he said, "but since you haven't, I'd really like to study it." I didn't know that Lane was particularly spiritual, but he said it wasn't the spiritual aspects, but about the drive of his soul.

"Drive of your soul?"

"Purpose," he said. "Marie says we all have a purpose in life, and this course helps us find it."

It was clear Lane enjoyed waitering, but he was never content. He felt something had to be missing, otherwise he would be higher on the economic ladder. He looked at himself as a second-class citizen, especially when he looked at the rest of us who made a whole lot more money.

"Marie says there are these things called spiritual codes that help you understand what you have been up to, where you are going, and where you *could* be going in your life. Maybe it can help me figure out what I should be doing with my life."

"Well, I guess it doesn't matter whether your birthday gift money goes toward an evening of wine or on the course. Sure!"

I told Lane I thought our purpose is to live a happy and joyful life, but Marie might have insights for him for his mission. This could very well help him be happier and more joyous. Either way, I knew he would love it.

Lane devoured that course as thoroughly as the Feng Shui course and came to the realization that his mission, that aspect of his soul that drives his life, is service. He's here to be of service to people. From that day on Lane beamed whenever he talked about being a waiter, and he became the best waiter at his restaurant, knowing that helping people with their sustenance and entertainment was infused into his DNA by his soul.

I then helped him realize that moving to a better restaurant would help with his tips. He picked out the restaurant he'd most like to be of service to, as he put it, applied, and got the job. "Nels," he said, "I exuded service and was exactly the type of server the restaurant needed." I smiled and congratulated him, knowing that the Persian blues probably had something to do with it, too.

Anyway, just as we were leaving Big Bob's, Quarry Girl began playing again. We moved to a table closer to her. It hadn't been cleared yet, but as soon as we sat down our waiter came over and cleaned it up. Tom said the waiter noticed the size of his tip. Lane said he was just being of service to us. I laughed. They were both right, I suppose.

Quarry Girl's voice was more suited for a coffeehouse than a barbecue joint, but she worked at connecting with people, and it came together. Even though I didn't know her, I was proud of her. It was cool seeing how she was stretching her boundaries by going out and playing where she was not necessarily welcomed, but making herself welcomed. Her smile, curly hair, and sweetness probably kept her from being shown the door. She was also a good musician, a good soul. Sue leaned to me saying, "I would imagine she's about the same age as Judy." I squeezed the soft area just above her knees.

"I'd like to dedicate the final song of the evening to a pod of friends who found me playing my flute in a quarry earlier today. I don't know whether they are creepy stalkers," she laughed, "or, like the rest of us, are the painted ponies captive on our carousel of life, showing up again and again. They've rented a motorhome and are out exploring the area, so for them I sing this Perry Como hit, 'Round and Round.'" She smiled toward us, looked down at her guitar, and... *Find a wheel and it goes round, round, round as it skims along with a happy sound. As it goes along the ground, ground, ground till it leads you to the golden ring.*

12

It Dawned on Me

ANOTHER BATTLE.

Tom talked with Big Bob about letting us overnight in his parking lot, and he was fine with it. I didn't want to drive, given how much I drank (every hour is a Saturday night with this group). I did drive us to the other end of the parking lot to get away from the smoker.

Lane lit his candles to cover the barbecue smells trapped in our clothes and hair and the smoke in the curtains of the beast, but QB Earl wanted to smell the smells all night. He loved his barbecue. Sue's eyes began to enlarge, hearing the tense tones, not wanting another episode like earlier today.

"Guys," I said, "let's do this. Lane blow out your candles. Tom rig a line outside. Everyone hang their clothes outside to air out. QB Earl, since you're sleeping in the back and Lane in the front, and since you got enough barbecue sauce in your beard to get you through the night, let Lane spritz the beds up front. Everyone agree?"

Soon we were all nestled in our beds. Tom and QB Earl were snoring within minutes, Lane was listening to a Paraliminal, Sue was flopped, and I was thinking how much I liked these guys, happy they are my family, my "pod" as Quarry Girl called us, and drifting off...until a police officer banged his flashlight on the RV door. Startled, I sat up quickly in bed, banging my head on the ceiling—damn, loft.

It took me a while to climb out, and he kept banging. And then I had to figure out how to unlock the door. Lane had been in charge of unlocking and opening the door, and he along with everyone else was dead to the world.

When I opened the door I was assaulted by an oversized Smith & Wesson super-bright flashlight blinding my eyes. I put my hands up to block the light.

"Hands down, please," he said.

"Can you get that out of my eyes?"

"Can I see your driver's license and proof of insurance?"

"What for, officer? What's the matter? What time is it?"

"You cannot park here."

"Big Bob said it was okay."

"Why would he say it was okay?"

"We'd been eating all of his meat and drinking all of his beer, and I suppose he didn't want us to drive, and probably wanted us to have lunch here tomorrow."

"This is private property."

"Yes, and the owner said we could park here."

"Are you arguing with me?" he asked.

"What? Of course not. This is private property and he said we could park here."

"Do you think I am stupid?" he spoke with angered intensity.

"No, I do not. Call Big Bob if you need too."

"Where's your driver's license? This is not a request. This is a demand. How many people do you have in here?"

"One thing at a time. Do you want my driver's license or do you want to know about people in here?"

He began to push past me, trying to get into the beast.

"Wait a minute," I said. "This is private property parked on private property. Get out of my motorhome. I will get you my driver's license." I somewhat surprised myself.

"Now," I said, once he got out. "Give me a minute." I turned, rolling my eyes, going back in for the license and insurance card. The cop seemed like someone who didn't want to work an overnight shift in a small town, having watched too much *NCIS, Nightwatch*, or one of those police shows.

I gave him my license and the card. "I'm going to call this in," he said.

Five minutes later he came back. "Everything checked out. But you should not be on private property without permission."

"We have permission."

"I do not see permission. Are you calling me a liar?"

"What? No I am not. Call Big Bob."

"He's not the owner."

"What? This is his place, and he said we could park here."

"But he doesn't own the place. He leases it."

"And he said there is no problem. Is there?"

"I don't like your attitude."

"I'm sorry. I'm tired. What do you want me to do?" I asked.

"Nothing. Have a good night." With that he turned away.

I stood there watching him for a good minute. What the

heck.

"What was that about?" asked Sue.

"Everything okay?" asked Lane.

"Hey, is everyone up? Why didn't you answer the door? Why didn't you come out to help me?" I asked.

Silence.

Those bozos.

I crawled back in bed, closed my eyes, and was wide awake from the surge of adrenaline. It gave me time to replay the events of the day, when it dawned on me. Quarry Girl changed the lyrics. She sang, "As it goes along the ground, ground, ground till it leads you to the golden ring."

That's not the lyrics. Perry Como sang "As it goes along the ground, ground, ground till it leads you to *the one you love.*" Golden ring. She knows about the hunt. She knows about the hunt.

13

Do You Have a Compass?

I OPENED MY EYES THINKING OF TEA. Lane's Persians were eight inches from mine. He was standing in front of my loft bed.

"Can I help you?"

"Where are we going today?"

The question took me fifteen years back to a nap on my sister's couch, when I opened my eyes to see my nephews Mit and Timmy sitting on the floor right in front of me with a note pad.

"Did you have the dream?" asked Mit, who on other days of the week might go by Mitchell. Timmy was always Timmy, and never a Tim or Timothy.

At lunch I had told the boys I began remembering a dream of buried treasure. "Hundreds of coins," I had said. "It was so real. I think it was real."

Mit and Timmy perked up. "Where is it?"

"I don't know."

"Think!"

"I am, but I don't know. I see a big rock."

"Is it near here?"

"I think so. Yes, it is somewhere near, but it's so cloudy, I can't see. Maybe if I can fall asleep again, I can fall back into that dream and figure it out."

My sister thought it was a ploy to get the kids to leave me alone so I could nap, and after doing the dishes, the boys were all too helpful to get me to the couch for a nap.

And what a beautiful nap I had. When I woke, I opened my eyes, and their eyes were eight inches from mine, just like Lane's.

"Did you dream?"

"Yes."

"Did you dream of the treasure." Mit sat with a pencil ready to write down everything I said.

"I did. I did. I know where it is."

"Where?" Mit asked.

"Do you have a compass?"

"Yes."

"Run and get it. Then follow the trail in the back until you come to a huge rock ledge. Gaze off in the distance where your compass says 210 degrees, and be careful not to fall. Did you get that?" I asked.

"Yes."

"Okay. Then go sixty-eight feet as the mockingbird flies. How far?"

"Sixty-eight feet," Mit repeated dutifully, writing it down.

"Good. There will be a big rock. Look at the base of its backside. That's it. Dig around with your hands."

And off they ran through the front door, coming back to

get the compass, leaving just as quickly, my sister yelling at them to close the door.

Ten minutes later the boys careened into the house, both holding a trove of dirt and coins in the belly of their T-shirts. They dumped them on the floor.

"Mom, mom, treasure! Uncle Nels! It was real treasure. Millions of dollars," said Mit.

"Get me a bucket," screamed Timmy.

"Look at this mess," responded my sister.

"Bucket. Mom, bucket. Come help us get all of the money. We are rich!"

My sister fell right into the boys' fantasy-come-true, running after them with an empty ice cream bucket for the boys' treasure, which I had buried for them earlier in the day when they were playing video games or something—it turned out more fun than I had imagined.

———

When we took off on our RV treasure hunt, I hadn't told anyone of our route. Every day I released the next location, giving the others the chance to solve it themselves. Now Lane, eight inches from my eyes, was ready for the next clue to the hunt, which was pretty much the next city on our route, which Lane surmised would help them solve the hunt. I was still surprised at how easy it was for me to solve it. Everything simply jumped off the page for me; I thought it would be fun to have everyone else solve it before we got there, so I told Lane where we were headed, and he grabbed his iPad for researching.

The rest of the RV was moving as slowly as I, none too quick to get on our way or even to know where we were going.

QB Earl hopped into the shower to wash the barbecue from his beard, asking me to wait for qigong practice until he was out.

Our runners Tom and Sue were still sleeping.

Qigong practice outside in the morning sun was beautiful, although the traffic noise wasn't quite like the gentle breeze in yesterday's meadow. I told QB Earl to imagine the traffic din driving him deeper and deeper into the peace of his practice.

I practice qigong because it feels so good, but I think QB Earl practices because he's afraid the cancer will come back. Everything I've read suggests that regular qigong practice dramatically shifts life to your favor, but QB Earl is afraid he's been cheating death.

Right out of college he and a dozen friends were tubing down the River of Pee. At least that's what it seemed to me.

Picture this, groups of twenty-something friends gather at a river and rent big rubber inner tubes from someone in a tumbledown shack.

When you go with friends, you tie the tubes together so you stay connected to share bum beer, chips, and Chips Ahoy. You drink the beer, tie your raft of tubes to other rafts of tubes (especially when you're running low on beer), laugh, laugh, laugh, and pee in the river as you float.

At some point you get out of the river, turn your tubes in to someone in another worn shack, and board a dilapidated, should-be-junked, cousin-of-the-beast school bus painted in wild colors to get back to your car and go home. Sun drenched. River drenched. Spent. And drunk.

QB Earl, back in the days when people simply called him Earl, floated with his friends down the River of Pee, being last in their train of tubes, drinking and laughing and being crazy along with everyone else, bobbing and bopping, bouncing and jouncing.

On one series of bounces his tube flipped over, sending him under water strapped to the tube with ropes and stuck in the hemp web, banging on boulders in the water, bloodying his forehead, bruising his chest, and battering his knees. He was trapped in a beating alliteration of pain, unbeknownst to the others in his floating carnival above.

Earl was forced to surrender to the river, flailing uncontrollably under the influence of beer, unable to panic, unable to command the circumstances, only able to experience the unfurling, gorgonizing drama, the whacking and thwacking of the river bottom, while his friends were oblivious to his absence.

Then he remembered reading a *Reader's Digest* article in his parent's basement bathroom on how feelings of warmth overcome people just before they drown. "I'm drowning," he thought. "This is it." And he felt comfortable with it, resigned to the end of life, wondering when the bright white light would appear, until he remembered he would be getting together with an old high school friend that Tuesday afternoon.

"She needs me," he thought. "She's having a tough turn in life." He grabbed his sunglasses that were smashed against his chest, thrust them skyward, piercing the water in a sign of defiance.

His friends noticed the hand coming from the water, clenching the sunglasses, and wondered a collective "What the heck!" Realizing Earl was in trouble, they pulled him up and eventually got him to the hospital, where he was outfitted with crutches to relieve pressure from his swollen knees—and with a new lease on life.

Ten, fifteen years later Earl's climbing an old basswood in his backyard to hang Christmas decorations.

A friend, who was the wife of a local television news anchor, had told him about decorations she created for a fundraising holiday tour of their house. She took dried grapevines and made balls about two feet across, wrapped them in white Christmas lights, and hung them from a huge tree in her backyard.

QB Earl, again only known as Earl, thought about the big basswood in his backyard, all of the grapevine along the fence, and, of course, "I can do that!"

Within a couple of weeks he had fashioned three grapevine balls that would hang from his basswood. He pulled out an old ladder and climbed 12 feet to the first branch to hang his first ball.

*Snap...crack...*and the branch fell, followed closely by the ladder and Earl. The ball bounced and rolled on the ground, the ladder bounced on the ground but stayed put, and Earl's head bounced on the ladder, with stars flying everywhere followed by blackness.

Sometime later he regained a semblance of consciousness, noticing the beauty of a light snowfall, feeling warm and comfortable, then realizing no one would find him until the snows melted in the spring.

He mustered the strength to get onto all fours and crawl into the house, where his then partner was sitting in the great room reading the morning paper.

Slightly panicked he asked, "What happened?"

Earl had no idea.

But he saw four computers on the floor in the great room.

"What are those doing here?"

"They are yours from the office."

"I would never bring them home."

"You had a major problem and brought them home to sort it out over the weekend."

"Why do I hurt so much?"

At that point his partner put two and two together. "You fell from the tree."

"What was I doing in the tree? It's snowing."

"Putting up Christmas decorations."

"But it's October thirtieth."

"Your friends Kip and Bonnie said they would be putting up theirs, and you thought 'Why wait until later,' so you wanted to put them out."

"Why do I hurt so much?"

"You fell from a tree."

"What was I doing in the tree?"

And the cycle continued, Earl without any short-term memory but a working memory for numbers.

"Call this number," he instructed.

"What is it for?"

"I don't know. Call it. Why do I hurt so much?"

It was Earl's chiropractor's office. They said to bring Earl in, and to the garage they went.

"Where is my car?" Earl asked, having noticed a white Subaru Outback.

"This is your car."

"No. I have a blue Honda Prelude."

"You sold it, and this is what you got."

"I would never buy a white car," said Earl.

"You got a good deal on it."

"Oh," said Earl. "Why do I hurt so much?"

Within a few hours they were at the hospital, the chiropractor having told them to get there immediately. Earl's body was poked, probed, and scanned, his wrist set and put in a cast, and his memory slowly returned.

He had just cheated death a second time.

His third cheat at death was the universe persistently trying to maim him, if not kill him, in three car accidents within three days.

Day one. The airport. He was picking up a friend. Earl opened the back of the car to load the luggage, and stepped aside to get the luggage when a taxi rammed the back of his car, missing him by inches.

The next day Earl's driving on the interstate when the cars in front of him slowed dramatically. He braked. The car behind him didn't. Instead it accelerated and changed lanes, leaving the cars behind him to plough in a chain reaction right into Earl.

But the car still worked, and on day three they headed to the collision center, stopping at the grocery. As they left the parking lot, a big pig of an SUV in front of them suddenly backed up, crawling over the hood of Earl's car.

Unharmed and unbruised, Earl got out of the car laughing uproariously at the third accident in three days. The young mother parachuted from her SUV and ran to Earl and his partner, yelling, "Are you okay? Why are you laughing?" Walking behind the car, seeing all of the damage from the previous two days, thinking she caused it, "Oh my Gawd! Did I do this? Are you okay? My husband will kill me."

Earl's car was in the shop for over a week, and he didn't want to drive anywhere, knowing he had shaken the grips of death for the third time.

And then his tumor, sepsis, and coma.

I told QB Earl that he was blessed, that he had great spiritual support, that there were many unseen helpers taking care of him, many ancestors looking over him

That may have calmed him down a little, but he seemed to be agitated more and more by the vagaries of life, like yesterday in the RV. He's practicing qigong to help keep the cancer away, because he's sure death will be knocking again and again.

Earl's one of the sweetest and kindest people I know who has been visited by so many close calls. It's no wonder he's concerned about the future. But given his ability to mix the best QB Cosmos on the planet, I'm thinking he's going to be just fine.

After qigong we drove to the diner for breakfast. After my shower, I joined them in the diner and their iPads slammed shut. Obviously they were not letting me in on their treasure hunting. I just smiled, ordered huevos rancheros, and soon an argument broke out over the best recording of "Stand by Me." Ben E. King or Mickey Gilley in *Urban Cowboy*, and all because Sue said, "Oh stop it. Stand by me." Before you know it we were watching YouTube videos.

Tom was the holdout, someone you would never peg as a country boy, but his youthful infatuation with the *Urban Cowboy* movie led his friend Michael and him to weld a fifty-five-gallon drum onto a giant spring and call it a mechanical bull for their summer party: Never Before, And Who Knows, We May Never Do It Again, Two Steppin, Country Crappin' Jamboree and Wing Ding. Country Crappin' for short.

Tom said the best part of Country Crappin' was when Michael's girlfriend-of-convenience, Shirley, rode the bull only to have the weld give way and the barrel and Shirley roll across the floor of the apartment building's party room.

Shirley was mad as hell, but a few month's later at a party in Tom's apartment, she offered a truce. Shirley was a hair stylist, the profession that everyone figured was the reason Michael dated her, because no one would want to sleep with her, and Michael's mane needed a lot of work, and on his salary, she was the best option. Anyway, she offered to cut Tom's hair. She set up a chair in the dining room, with the partiers in the living room.

Shirley meticulously cut Tom's hair, only to do a whack job on the left side, which no one saw. She laughed and laughed and left the party. Tom had to go to another hairstylist the next day to have his hair buzz cut, removing Shirley's lack of artistry. "If the design was cool, I would have kept it," he said.

"But weren't you pissed?" I had asked.

"Not really. She was not all that bright, and besides it would grow back within a few weeks," said Tom.

Tom and Michael were the Dynamic Duo, lunching every Saturday on hotdogs and popcorn at the neighborhood Olds dealer and crashing wedding receptions nearly every Saturday evening. "We got to eat," Tom would say. "We got to drink," Michael would say.

Tom was in his early entrepreneurial days, having to make do. To earn money he'd telemarket heating and air conditioning systems. "Hi, this is Tom Johnson with such-and-such heating and air conditioning. Next Tuesday we are at the home of someone down the street doing a free heating and air conditioning survey, and I am happy to have the technician stop by your house if you are available." He was consistently the top lead generator, because everyone loved him on the phone, and that gave him the money to keep trying his business ideas. It took ten years before one finally caught on, and then another ten years to make serious money, but it was Michael who had his back during the early days.

One of Tom's earliest business successes came during the first few weeks of telemarketing. He realized his middle name, Tom, was less likely to stop people than his given name, Tyrone. "Ty-what?" they would ask. Homeowners were so fixated on the name that he couldn't get the appointment. He'd later reflect, "I don't know whether it was prejudice or ignorance, but it all went away when I used the name, Tom. I'd like to think it was ignorance, but I don't think it was."

No Dynamic Duo is complete without the third, making The Three Musketeers. And that third was Carla May whose husband, Bill, had a hard time with Tom and Michael but rolled with it.

Tom and Carla May invented Wine Tennis. They were so bad at tennis that whenever anyone would walk by, they would go to the net and talk until the intruder walked on past. One day Carla May said it sure would be nice to have a glass of wine. The next day Tom showed up with an airpot of cheap but cold zinfandel, and every time someone would walk by, they would go to the net and have a glass of wine. Paper cup of wine, that is.

Soon, tennis was only the cover.

Soon, they gave up tennis all together and just drank wine every afternoon.

That was perhaps why it took Tom longer to have one of his businesses take off. Too much wine on sunny afternoons.

That was the same tennis court that got the police to visit Michael and Tom the first time.

The sidewalk to the court was typical. One concrete section after another, and *voila*, a tennis court. But two sections of sidewalk before the court, an extra section jutted off to the right for no apparent reason.

Tom and Michael surmised it was for wheelchair parking, so they made a sidewalk-sized stencil and spray-painted a wheelchair on the sidewalk so everyone would know the place was reserved for those in wheelchairs.

The next time the police visited the two was in response to posters tacked throughout the apartment complex signed by the Highfence Revolutionary Council. Highfence was the name of the complex, and the Council was formed to scare the paperboy into delivering the morning papers in a timely manner.

The third time the police visited the two was when super glue had been squirted into the lock on the door to the apartment complex office. Carla May came to their rescue, saying she saw someone by the door late that night.

Today Tom couldn't remember why they squirted the glue, but he figured it had to have been justified. Carla May's only comment back then was, "Boys! Good job." No one really liked the managers.

Their adventures were countless, including double dates where Michael cheated on Shirley, and afternoons-a-cycling when they would have been better off at home. One time they cycled twelve miles to visit one of Michael's side girlfriends. She gave them a bag of homemade chocolate chip cookies as they headed home. Coming down a hill, Michael needed to brake to avoid a car, and he squeezed the right brake lever a little too tight, sending him over the handlebars.

Cookies were everywhere.

Seven miles later, Tom tipped over and skidded through a

residential intersection. He had fallen asleep at the handlebars.

The two bloodied friends made it back to Tom's apartment where they took turns cleaning dirt out of their wounds. Whiskey made it all feel better.

"It stung like hell," recalled Tom. "All I had was straight bum whiskey, no sour, nothing to mix it with. In those days I had no idea about good booze like Buffalo Trace Bourbon. I bought the cheapest, and it really was bad without the mix, but we needed to do something for the pain. We shot a half dozen shots." Michael missed his work the next day. Tom just slept, leaving his entrepreneurial duties to later in the day.

———

Soon we finished our meal at the diner and were back in the beast ready for our ninety-two-mile trip northward, me burping huevos rancheros. First, a stop for snacks, sandwich fixin's, and booze (Meyer's Dark Rum and Bacardi Piña Colada Mix—QB Earl packed a blender).

We're really not the boozers we appear to be, but we're on vacation, on a mission to find treasure, and we like each other and we like booze. Heck, as I'm tidying up this chapter, I'm drinking a glass of Lido Bay Seven Seas Chardonnay.

14

The Spy Who Drinks Chardonnay

DURING OUR HOUR AND A HALF RIDE to our next destination, Tom googled up a beautiful canoe trip for us and found a couple of canoes for rent. QB Earl reminded us that the blender for piña coladas wasn't battery powered, so we needed to stop for a lunch wine.

I pulled the beast into a large parking lot that had a liquor store attached, but no one wanted to go in. "It's too cheap. They won't have any decent wine."

"Yah, but we have easy parking here," I said. "Let's go in."

"Nah, let's go down the highway to the next one," said Tom looking at his phone. "It's a wine shop-pe," adding a second syllable to Wine Shoppe.

"Wine Shop-pe," said Lane in deadpan.

"Wine Shop-pe!" exclaimed Sue.

I said, "This thing is so difficult to park, let's just try this out."

So everyone got off with me, went into the liquor store, Lane bounding ahead and coming back saying, "Just beer and booze, let's get out of here, it stinks."

The store stunk something sour. It took a couple of quick snorts to get the smell out of my nose.

They were right. The Wine Shoppe was nicer, and even nicer still was their wine sale. The Lido Bay bin was empty, so we grabbed a couple of bottles of some other chardonnay—actually a mixed case because the prices were so good.

The gal in front of us at the cash register had two bottles of Lido Bay. She had taken the last ones!

"Hey, you snookered the last Lido Bay!" I exclaimed, with a smile in my voice.

She turned around to us, saying, "Sorry, would you…" Stopping in her tracks. Us freezing in place.

"Quarry Girl?" I said, slowly.

"What are you doing here?" she asked defensively. "Hey wait, Quarry Girl? What do you mean by that?"

"That's what we call you. We don't know your real name," I said.

"Miss, that would be $57.46. Can I see some ID?"

"Ah, excuse me." She handed the clerk a credit card and driver's license.

"What is your name? I'm Nels, this is Lane, QB Earl, and that guy over there is Tom." Looking around, "I don't know where Sue is."

"Ahhh, are you following me?" she asked hesitantly. "Or is this just a coincidence?"

"Gawd no," said QB Earl. "We're certainly not following you. Are you following us?"

"What? I was here first," said Quarry Girl.

I stared at her, thinking of the lyrics she changed. *Till it leads you to the golden ring.* Is she on the treasure hunt? Is she simply traveling to the treasure, or is she spying on us? Is she working alone? Does she have partners? How did she get in the store before we did if she was following us?

15

Jus de Pomme de Terre

"I DON'T KNOW," said QB Earl a little panicked. "I'm concerned. What if she is following us?"

"Calm down a bit," I said, paddling one of our two canoes, thinking of the changed lyrics, but not wanting to set off QB Earl.

"I am calm. Don't tell me to calm down. But what if she is in the hunt?"

"Well," I said, "It's a game. Who cares. It just adds intrigue."

"But the prize money is a lot of money," said Lane.

"It's not ours yet. I'm not even sure I am completely right."

"Yah, but I was hoping to pay for my share of expenses on this trip from the prize money," said Lane, perhaps thinking about his tip jar.

"Should we be following her?" asked Tom. "Just in case?"

"That's an interesting idea. But we don't know where she is

right now," I said.

"Do we know her name?" Sue asked. "Did she ever give us her name? I don't think so. I'd remember."

"You asked once," said QB Earl looking at me, "and she never told us."

"Did she give her name to anyone else?" I asked. "Lane you spent the most time with her. You talked with her at the quarry."

"Yah, but I don't remember if she gave her name."

"How come?" challenged QB Earl.

"Well, I didn't know I would be quizzed. Heck, I didn't know that she'd keep popping up."

"Did anyone see what car she was driving?"

"You know," said Sue, "she's been consistent in her story about being filmed for a homemade documentary. I think it would be fun to be part of a documentary. There's a lot in my life..."

Lane rolled his eyes, something he gleefully picked up from me, the master of the eye roll. "They already filmed you. You are part of the documentary."

"But where was her cameraman in the store?" asked Tom, ignoring her docu-wishes.

"Maybe the shooter was out in the car, at a grocery store, scouting a location, who knows," responded Sue, taking the shifting conversation in stride.

"Good point," I said.

Just then someone scolded us in French, probably for being too loud. They were in another canoe coming up from behind. Apparently we were noisy in addition to being slow.

The only French I know is *Jus de pomme de terre*. I speak it convincingly whenever anyone talks about the French language, speaks French, or when it simply seems appropriate.

I say it with whatever inflection the situation calls and with whatever meaning I want.

With exasperation, *Jus de pomme de terre.*

With surprise, *Jus de pomme de terre!*

With the of-course-I-speak-French attitude, *Jus de pomme de terre.*

With no-no-not-that, *Jus de pomme de terre.*

It means *Juice of the Apple of the Earth.* Which is *Juice of the Potato.* Which is *Potato Juice.* Which is what captured me, *Vodka.*

So all I could say to the French canoeists was *"Jus de pomme de terre"* with a sharp twist of defiance. I looked firmly in their eyes and turned away.

There's no telling what went through their French-squeezed brains as California wine squeezed through our veins. If you can't mess with your fellow human beings, who can you mess with?

We just sat there for a bit. Calming down. Taking in the beauty. Letting the Frenchies paddle ahead. I did feel a little sheepish for losing my cool.

"I thought I said I wasn't going to haul around any more heavy bottles of wine," said QB Earl, moving the backpack of wine and ice.

"That's why we got chardonnay instead of champagne," I quipped. "The bottles are lighter."

"Besides, you are in a canoe," said Lane in a fit of in-your-face logic. "What do you care?"

"Just open a bottle," said Sue.

"Good idea," I said. "But I'm thinking we should hightail it out of here after the treasure."

"Can you drink in a boat?" asked Tom.

"Just open a bottle," said Sue.

"So no one else thinks we should just go after the treasure?" I asked again.

"What do your rubies say?" asked Lane.

"Just open a bottle," said Sue. "We can talk about speeding up the trip later. It's still a couple of hours before the rental place will meet us for the canoes." That made sense, but I still had a little anxiety about Quarry Girl. I guess if we weren't the ones to win the treasure, she certainly seemed nice enough.

It took a couple of minutes to get the two canoes side by side, and then to stabilize the one in which the uncorking would occur.

"Careful," said Tom, as the canoes rocked a little more than was comfortable.

"Tippy Canoe and Tommy, too," smiled Lane.

Tom glared back.

"We should have brought screw-top bottles," said QB Earl.

"Too easy," said Lane, our professional bottle opener, as the cork slipped from the bottle.

And within a couple of minutes we realized that you cannot drink wine and paddle a canoe at the same time, so Sue pulled out the sandwiches. "Luckily we made them in the beast."

"Luckily there are no bugs," I said.

We sat gazing at a beautiful big tree across the water.

"That's the biggest tree I've seen," said Lane. "And a bit odd looking."

"It's gotta be, what, two hundred years old?"

"It's a bicentennial tree," said Tom.

"Did you make that up?" asked Sue.

"What's a bicentennial tree?" asked Lane.

"I don't know. One that's been around two hundred years?"

"Looks like one. Let's call it that," said Lane.

"That's my second bicentennial tree," said Tom. "We were under the first one roasting cinnamon and sugar donuts during the Basic Bicentennial Bop Back to Babbitt."

Our heads all turned to Tom with what-was-that looks. In impeccable cadence he regaled us back to the summer of his freshman year with a half-dozen college friends heading to his hometown's bicentennial celebration.

His minimotorcade pulled up to his family home where in the driveway glittered letters were taped to the basketball back-board, proclaiming, "Welcome B.B.B.B.T.B", with crepe paper flowers dotting the rim of the hoop.

They honked their car horns and out from the neighbor's garage came a brass band of his sister on a bassoon, two neighbor girls on a trumpet and trombone, and the neighbor boy on a drum. It was high school band at its worst, small town living at its best. Right on cue, his mother, draped in a garish red, white, and blue apron, carried out a platter of sloppy joes. "A sandwich is a sandwich, but a Manwich is a meal." And then his dad and his bucket of beers and Uncle Bernie with his beer opener.

Sometime later Tom's dad gave the college buddies their camping instructions for that evening. Benny would light the lantern, Steve would light the fire, Tom, Rick, and Beat Darryl would pitch the tent, and Phil would unload the sleeping bags and food, while Trent managed to get by with no duties. After loading the camping gear into the cars, off they went, stopping by the Legion for more beer. As they walked in, Tom's other sister led the bar in cheers, and the band rocked their version of "At the Hop." *Let's go to the Bop. Let's go to the Bop. Let's go to the Bop. Come on, let's go to the Bop.*

After a few hours and twenty miles they pulled into their campsite in the national park among the old growth trees, Benny out cold in the backseat and no one able to light the lantern. They all liked the idea of camping, but no one had actually done it before, and Tom's dad had not crossed-trained anyone for the lantern.

Steve was sober enough to light the campfire, but apparently not skilled enough. How long does it take for a committee of drunks to light a campfire? Just over an hour. And a little longer than that for Tom, Rick, and Beat Daryl to pitch the tent.

Morning came and Beat Darryl screamed at a claw hammer he pulled from under his sleeping bag, which he had apparently slept on all night. "I thought there was a rock under the tent, and there wasn't room to move my sleeping bag away from it. I didn't sleep all night."

"Where did a hammer come from?" asked Steve.

"I used it to pound in the tent stakes," said Beat Darryl.

"And then you put it under your sleeping bag?" asked Steve, rolling over to sleep some more.

Tom said it was hard for everyone not to laugh. Beat Darryl had earned his name, which came from his midnight ritual at college. He'd crank open his fourth-floor dorm window and yell out, "It is twelve o'clock, and you are all beat," the last word reverberating through the courtyard and bouncing out into the valley below.

Phil slipped out of the tent to get breakfast ready, but apparently no one had actually put the food in the cars, other than for a box of cinnamon and sugar donuts. The guys roasted the donuts over the embers, Rick looking up and saying, "My Gawd that's a big tree," and Tom saying, "It's a bicentennial tree."

16

Stations of the Frogs

As we drifted down the river, Tom pointed out interesting trees, including a majestic evergreen he had in his backyard.

He also has eight 880-pound stone frogs.

Who doesn't, right?

They were souvenirs from a trip to Bali.

I come back from a trip with perhaps a T-shirt. Tom comes back with the beginnings of a private Easter Island.

Two of his friends invited a small group to a lush and tropical compound of five houses they rent every year on the Badung Strait, just off the Indian Ocean. You walk onto the tropical property through a gauntlet of gigantic fat and happy frogs carved from dark gray lava, each playing a different Balinese musical instrument.

"I could hear them play every time I walked by," Tom said. "It was that distinct metallic rhythm heard all over the island.

There were four frogs on each side for about fifteen yards. They seemed to watch you as you walked. So joyful."

On the eighth night in Bali he dreamt of the frogs coming home with him and sitting in a labyrinth on his property. A labyrinth is like a maze for people who don't like games, because there are no dead ends or trick passages. Just a pleasant, circuitous walk.

For the past few years Tom had talked about building labyrinths. He sketched four designs for four different areas on his property, but he never pulled the trigger. It was always next year, and he always talked about them. He bought a dozen books on labyrinths with hopes to find an explanation for his labyrinth-brain affliction. It would often puzzle him why he never would build one, thinking perhaps it would be too much work.

He woke up that morning in Bali and sketched the labyrinth from his dream, complete with vestibules along the paths where the frogs would be stationed. Stations of the Cross, if you will, not of suffering, but the release of suffering, an expression of joy, so Stations of the Frog. And he called it a Frogyrinth.

Over breakfast he told his friends of the dream and showed them the Frogyrinth design. Within the hour they had piled into the van to drive around Bali to find duplicate stone frog statues.

That wasn't too far out of the realm of possibility, because the Balinese are a people of creative expression. There are hundreds, if not thousands, of stone carvers, with shops along every road filled with life-size stone statues of lava, limestone, sandstone, and other rock. Most of the statues were of Balinese mythical creatures and gods, like the fierce-looking Barong, king of the good spirits and enemy of Rangda, the demon queen. But you could find most anything you wanted. Except for fat and happy frogs playing Balinese musical instruments.

The next day as they rode elephants at the Bali Zoo, Tom thought of frogs. And so did everyone else. Where could they find frogs?

Friends who live on Bali joined them for dinner that evening, and they all talked about the quest for frogs. One of their friends said, "I know a carver. Let's get him pictures of these and see if he can carve duplicates." Tom quickly corrected her, "Cousins. Not duplicates. Cousins."

Five months later, eight frogs and a Barong, for good juju, were making their way across the ocean. Tom, with the help of eager labor off Craigslist, laid out the Frogyrinth on his property and planted 226 bushes in the areas between the paths of the Frogyrinth.

Everyone was overwhelmed by the scope of the project except for Tom, who simply did it without batting a lash. The labyrinth plans of the previous few years had simply been released in an unending flow of energy and clear thinking.

The frogs had been offloaded in the Port of Long Beach and held hostage by a greedy warehouse man wanting more money, thinking they had a chump in Tom.

Greedy Warehouse Man: They are delicate statues. We should truck them by air cushion so they don't break.

Tom: They are stone. Ship them by rail. If they break, they are fully insured.

Greedy Warehouse Man: We paid a crating company to add more support to the crates, because they were falling apart, and you owe us an additional nine hundred dollars.

Tom: The shipper from Bali ships these statues all over the world. They know how to crate the statues. I am not paying a penny more. Besides, they are insured.

Greedy Warehouse Man: We cannot stack the statues in the rail cars, so you owe us double to pay for all of the empty space above each crate.

Tom: The shipper from Bali already scammed me by double-charging me, so I paid for the space above the damn crates.

Greedy Warehouse Man: They admitted to double-charging you?

Tom: Yes, and they felt bad about you wanting to double-double-charge me. They have their limits.

The frogs arrived at a rail yard about forty miles from Tom's house and caught a flatbed truck out to his place.

The truck driver told Tom to take his time as he offloaded his eight frogs and one Barong with his forks. (Apparently, when you live in the country you have man toys such as a forklift.)

The first 880-pound frog was fifteen feet in the air when Tom wanted to set it on the ground. The center of gravity shifted, and the machine and the frog lunged forward and down about a foot. The back of the machine went up a foot. It started to teeter-totter. The truck driver ran toward Tom, jumping on the machine to add stabilizing weight.

Tom had a similar issue with each frog, although nothing was as dramatic or breath-stopping as the first.

The driver cautioned him to go slow saying, "My boss said to take as much time as needed. It's important that the Buddhas are treated with respect."

"Buddhas?" Tom questioned.

"My boss looked in one of the crates and saw they are all stone statues of Buddha."

Tom said, "No, they are frogs. Fat, happy, and Buddhalike, but frogs."

The driver looked at him. "Well, she thinks they are Buddhas so take your time."

A few minutes later the driver told Tom they had a ceremony when loading the truck.

Tom gave solace, saying one of the frogs, with a Buddha belly, was sitting in the lotus position.

Tom's ongoing story about the frogs had me asking about the frogs as I would someone's dog, and when I first saw them I was instantly and immediately smitten, so much so I offered to *fly* the frogs with him, the harrowing and muscle-strapping process of raising the stone monoliths onto concrete pedestals in the Frogyrinth. Over the course of a few weeks we wrapped heavy-duty tow straps around each frog and lifted them by other straps attached to Tom's forklift. They were literally flown into place on the pedestals. Remember, these were 880-pound stone frogs, not cute robin redbreasts flittering about, which meant we were just inches away from crushing someone's arm or smashing a frog to smithereens. As it was, I stood up once banging my head into one of the forks, seeing stars just like in the cartoons and saying a choice word or two. The first frog took ninety minutes to fly, because we really didn't know what we were doing. By the time we were flying the final frog a few weekends later at the dedication party, it took only five minutes. We had it down. We could have gone into the frog-flying business.

On that Balinese beach one morning out in front of their compound, Tom had met a young gal playing a Balinese bamboo flute.

When we first met Quarry Girl playing her flute, Tom had said she played as enchantingly as the gal in Bali, who, as wonders would have it, lives in the first town over from Tom's home. She had been vacationing in Bali, and she'll be joining us at the Frogyrinth Dedication Ceremony the weekend after we return from our treasure hunting adventure.

As I lie in bed tonight, I hear an army of frogs croaking up a storm out here where we ended our day's canoe ride.

We weren't planning on overnighting here, but we couldn't get the rolling beast started. The RV rental center was not answering the phone, and the after-hours emergency number was disconnected. I guess that's one way to keep repair expenses down.

My Gawd those frogs are loud.

17

Made Fresh Each Morning

"AT LEAST WE DIDN'T TRY beating Quarry Girl to the treasure," said Lane.

We just looked at him, drinking coffee, sipping tea, waiting for the mechanic.

"How do you figure?" asked QB Earl, in his curmudgeonly way.

"Well, then we would be pissed that the RV broke. Now we're just enjoying the morning," said Lane.

Sue uncovered a hidden box of glazed doughnuts. "I snuck away while you guys were in the wine shop. I mean Wine Shoppe. I love glazed doughnuts." Looking at me, "I knew you and Tom would never get them yourselves."

"But we will still eat them."

"We have a sickness," said Tom.

"Enough," said Lane reaching over for his.

"You'll love the label," said Sue. "Our ingredients are natural. Our glaze, fillings, and pastries homemade. Our dough is made fresh each morning by our in-house baker. His home is upstairs, but his heart is in this box. He uses no preservatives or artificial anything. He engages in no random activities. He simply bakes wholesome goodness. For you."

"I bet he's fat," smiled Tom.

"As a loaf of bread," said Sue.

"Is it too early for piña coladas?" asked QB Earl.

"Let's go for a walk first," said Tom.

"After this wholesome goodness," said Lane.

18

The Butterscotch Clipper

"I HAPPEN TO KNOW RVs don't just break down," said the rental guy speaking loud enough for everyone within twenty feet of the phone to hear. "They are well maintained. They are workhorses. They do not break down."

"This broke down," I said.

"What did you do to it?"

"Nothing. We spent the afternoon canoeing, came back to our rolling palace, and it did not start."

"Do you know how much this mechanic costs me?" he said screeching across country.

"That's not my fault."

"And it's mine? You are driving it."

"No I'm not. It won't drive."

"What the friggin'. Stop messin' with me." Blue lightning all over the place.

The mechanic took the phone from me. "Hey, cool it. It's the fuel pump. It's not their fault, and it's not your fault. That fuel pump simply failed. It shouldn't have, but it did. I need to have it towed. The new fuel pump will take two or three days to get here. And it's a day or two to repair. You're looking at a couple of thousand."

More blue lightning.

The mechanic joined our eye rolls.

The RV guy agreed to the repairs. "I need a credit card to proceed," smiled the mechanic.

More blue lightning.

Ultimately, the RV guy gave us a refund for the rental. Of course, he left us stranded, but our mechanic knew of a guy in town with an RV to rent. He gave me a lift, while QB Earl began the transmogrification sequence of blender button pushing. Chop. Mix. Puree. Liquefy. *Voila!* Piña coladas. Luckily the generator still worked.

As we drove through a residential area, the mechanic said, "Don't get too excited about the RV."

"Don't worry," I said, "my expectations are way low at this point."

"That's not what I mean," he said, as we turned the corner in straight view of a 1948 *Flxible Clipper*, a fully restored and converted bus of classic luxury, with its smiley face front end, curved panoramic windshield, high-polished chrome streaking around, and tasty butterscotch baked-enamel finish. As we drove to it, a curved-down bubble-butt behind came into view. "Get too excited and he'll jack up the price."

When the old man climbed down from the bus, I thought of Charles Dickens and "every wrinkle but a notch in the quiet calendar of a well-spent life."

He smiled broadly, stretching out his huge hands to shake mine. "I hear you're a pickle."

"A pickle?"

"Yup, a pickle in a pickledicament."

"I guess you could say that. I'm a pickle-in-a-pickledicament."

"Well, welcome, I have just the beauty for you," he said, turning sideways, gesturing widely to the butterscotch loveliness. "I present, the Butterscotch Clipper."

The mechanic nudged me, whispering, "Get that shit-eatin' grin off your face."

Inside, rich dark wood followed the curve of the ceiling, a grain I was not familiar with, complementing the wood floor, leather couch, two beautiful side chairs covered in jewel tones of wool fabric, updated chrome-coated kitchen, four curtained sets of bunk beds, a pounded copper wall on the back bubble butt, which the old man informed me was a "bullet butt," not a "bubble butt." The bathroom was a piece of art. Three circular modules, like leaves on a clover, one for the shower, one for the toilet, and the center for the sink. Tight, but spacious. Absolutely amazing.

"How much?" I asked.

Reverse sticker shock.

"That's too low," I said.

The mechanic turned quickly to me, eyes popping out.

"Nah," the old man said. "We're just so happy someone can enjoy it. No one around here will rent it. They're afraid they'll wreck it. You know, it's not like you can go out and buy a replacement."

"I wonder how we can get it back to you after our trip."

"In one piece, please."

I looked at him, sliding one eyebrow up and the other down.

He smiled.

"I've thought of that. The wife and I need to visit our son down where you're from. We'll meet you there. She'll drive the car, and I'll take this back."

"You sure?"

"Absolutely. Do you have cash?"

"Yes, I do," I said, watching the mechanics eyes pop again.

"Good, I'll take one thousand now and the rest when we know how many days you have it."

"Fair enough," I said as I pulled out a wad of twenties rubber banded together. Tom always travels with a bundle of cash, and I had the foresight to ask him for it before I left them behind with their coconuted rum.

"Got anything there for me?" asked the mechanic.

"Get yours from the rental center," I said furling both brows. He smiled.

"One last thing before you go," said the old man. He pulled a bag of butterscotch candies from his pocket. "It's sort of a theme around here."

"Any Tuaca?" I asked.

"Tuaca?"

"It's a butterscotch-tasting liqueur."

"Well, that's new to me. I'll head on over to the liquor store with this wad of money and check it out." The old man smiled, squeezing the wad.

"This is good living," I said aloud as I drove away. I couldn't wait to see everyone's expressions. Hopefully they saved a piña colada for me.

19

Gru-worthy

LANE'S WIND SPINNER OF MESMERISM hung frozen in time from the beast's unfurled awning, wanting to twirl backwards to reexamine what appeared to be a ripple in the space-time continuum. The Butterscotch Clipper came to rest.

Playing cards dripped from the hands of Sue, Lane, and QB Earl. Tom, partially hidden behind a tree, steadily lowered his phone. Slow motion grins took center stage on their faces. They could see me beaming my pearly whites in the driver's seat.

Then like kids on Christmas morning, they tore into their new present. QB Earl sat in one of the side chairs, his hands rubbing back and forth on the fabriced arms. Lane looked up at the wood ceiling, his mouth agape, walking toward the back, running his hands on the chrome in the kitchen, through the drapes of the bunks, and to the shiny pounded copper back wall. Tom, feeling the ceiling, looking at the kitchen, opening the drawers and doors, and finding a blender, finally said to QB Earl, "Make up some more piña coladas. We got some celebrating to do." Sue just stood there with her hands on the rubied curves of her hips, mouth smirking like Bette Midler, "Where the hell did you get this?! It's beautiful. It's a glistening antique. Wow. Where did you get it?"

I stood up and made the same sweeping gesture as the old man. "Welcome to the Butterscotch Clipper!"

I paused for effect. "Our new home, our version of the Flying Anglia, sans the Whomping Willow."

Sue yelped, "To the Butterscotch Clipper!"

"Butterscotch Clipper" cheered everyone. QB Earl stopping himself short to squirrel out and fetch the makings for more piña coladas.

The original RV was a cheap piece of mechanical fecal material. It smelled, it was cheesy ugly, and it ran like a worn-out Chevy. But what do you expect when renting an RV at the last minute during peak season. It was not *Gru-worthy*.

My friend D.J., who I love dearly, is not the social type, and would never join an expedition like this, although we'd all enjoy his company. Years ago he discovered a treat he shared with me. We gave it the nickname *Gru*. But because it is hard to come by and awfully expensive, we indulge for only the most Gru-worthy moments.

It's come to mean anything out-of-the-ordinary special, at least in conversations between him and me. We swore not to tell anyone else about it—not sure why other than it is a secret he and I share, it's kind of a blood brother thing, and now here I am blabbing wide open in a book, but the Butterscotch Clipper is worthy of the breach. It is Gru-worthy.

Not much in life is Gru-worthy. All right, everything really is Gru-worthy when you look at the joyous beauty all around us. We do live in a magnificent world and life can really be good. But that's a more esoteric look at life. Gru-worthiness is base, appealing to the everyday aesthetics of life.

Tom's Frogyrinth is Gru-worthy, gasp-worthy, actually. A gas station is not. You don't stand looking at a pump in full admiration. The Butterscotch Clipper is Gru-worthy. It's gorgeous. Every detail. It's nothing like what you would find in one of those million dollar RVs. Those are a bit too fancy, too made-up. They belong in a magazine. They probably don't even run. They are made just to look at. And never sit on one of those chairs, because it probably isn't comfortable.

The Butterscotch Clipper's leather sofa is perfectly proportioned to the space, and it has the perfect balance between a soft jacket leather and something to withstand RV users. The kitchen looks like it grew there. It belongs there. Most RV kitchens look like they were assembled in a factory, shoved through the tiny door of the RV, and hot-glued to the wall.

After some time, an outpouring of purple rain, and more piña coladas, we got all of our goods out of the beast and stowed in the Butterscotch Clipper. We're spending another night before heading out, primarily because I don't feel like driving.

We'll head into town for dinner and bug out early in the morning. I told everyone the name of our next destination, and they are on their phones trying to figure out where we are ultimately heading to find the treasure. I feel a bit funny they are leaving me out of the conversations, because I'd love to watch their processes and maybe even give them hot and cold signals, but ultimately they want to do it on their own.

What's a skinny boy to do.

Qigong. That's what I'll do. I'll go find a big fat tree and practice qigong in front of it. The energy of a tree is so powerful. I'll let the others search for the legendary hoard of gold and jewels, a chest of swag from a pirate-themed parallel universe, "Yo-ho-ho, and a bottle of rum!"

Hmmm. You know what I'll wait for. A piña colada.

After qigong.

20

Invoking the Law of Attraction

My Gawd, last night's sleep was good. The mattresses were top-bunk.

All right. I try to stay away from puns, but they were really comfortable. No smells, other than slight wisps of Lane's famous homemade candles. He had promised to tone them down, because there weren't other smells we needed to cover up.

Even the ventilation system worked slick, and we didn't have to put up with QB Earl's farts. Of course, we did give him the top bunk closest to the vent. We drew straws who had to sleep below him, just in case of heavy currents. Had I lost, I would have pulled the "I paid for Butterscotch Clipper, I don't sleep there" card. Tom would have claimed it was his cash. Sue would have pulled the gender card. Poor Lane. But he is the youngest and probably has the strongest immune system. QB

Earl has been eating pretty much the same as the rest of us. We think he hasn't fully recovered from the surgeries yet. The body is still expelling toxins.

The bathroom in the Butterscotch Clipper is Gru-worthy. It is a piece of engineering art with the three circular modules. It was made for my body. That old man had his act together. I hope Tom buys this. I would, but I live in the city. He has all of the space in the country. Of course, he might say, "Buy it and I'll let you store it here in exchange for using it," but I hope he doesn't think of that.

I get to experience the Butterscotch Clipper. I don't have to own it. I get to experience the Butterscotch Clipper. I don't have to own it. I get to experience the Butterscotch Clipper. I don't have to own it. Maybe if I repeat it enough I'll believe it.

Behind the wheel, it's smooth sailing. What a beautiful sunrise. Clear skies. We've been so lucky on the trip with the weather. Sue and QB Earl have their bio-chainsaws running. Lane is making tea and coffee. Tom is finding stuff for us to do when we land. It's fun driving. Everyone gives us second glances. Kinda like the Flying Anglia. I'm surprised at how smooth it rides. The instrument panel is fresh out of the 1940s. So cool looking. Fun to drive. I'm sure the 114 miles will be a joy.

Lane brought me English Breakfast and a little bowl of raw almonds, walnuts, and cashews. Life cannot be better.

"Wanna go bicycling?" asked Tom.

"Sure," said Lane.

"If we can get decent bikes," I said. "My butt isn't ready for cheap seats."

"There's an excellent rental shop about forty-five miles north of where we are heading, with a great route along the river and through a gorgeous park."

"Can't we rent bikes where we are headed? There's got to be good trails there."

"Yup," said Tom, "At least one really good trail, but there is no place to rent a decent bike."

"Okay. I'm in. Ask Sue and QB Earl when they are up, and let's do it. Have you found a breakfast place yet?"

"About an hour from here," said Tom.

"Perfect," I said, sipping the tea.

Since the Butterscotch Clipper is a reconditioned bus with the door directly opposite of the driver's seat, the only place for someone to keep the driver company is in a jump seat slightly on the edge of the driver's peripheral vision. It wasn't conducive for conversation, which is probably what the old man wanted. A respite from the wife.

Lane sat in the jump seat and leaned forward. "Why hadn't you invoked the Law of Attraction earlier?"

"What?" I asked.

"Why didn't you invoke the Law of Attraction earlier to get the Butterscotch Clipper from the beginning?"

I laughed, "I hadn't thought of it!"

"How could you not think of something as powerful as the Law of Attraction when you first saw the beast?"

"Probably too busy hoping you'd bring your smell-be-gone candles."

Lane was right. I should have thought of it. I use it all of the time. Ask. Believe. Receive. It's the old adage that you attract what you focus on.

Years ago I came across a quote in a brochure. I remember it so well. "What you vividly imagine, ardently desire, sincerely believe, and enthusiastically act upon must inevitably come to pass." In essence, that's the Law of Attraction, which I really hadn't heard about until *The Secret* movie came out.

It had become my mantra. "What you vividly imagine, ardently desire, sincerely believe, and enthusiastically act upon must inevitably come to pass." And I think it helped me find much of the success I enjoy in life.

At some point when I wasn't getting enough writing gigs or when they didn't pay well or when I wasn't thrilled with what I wrote, I made a list of everything that paid buckets of money and that I thoroughly loved. It became abundantly clear: I wasn't imagining vividly enough. I wasn't desiring ardently enough. I wasn't believing sincerely enough and certainly not acting enthusiastically enough.

I realized that when I had scored with the perfect gig, I was fully engaged with passion, belief, and enthusiasm not only about what I was doing, but during those periods of time.

And when things were thin, I was disengaged again, in the writing and, more importantly, in my life. I wasn't connecting with life, so I was attracting writing gigs that matched that energy of my life.

So I began spending eight minutes every morning—don't ask me why eight minutes, I probably read it somewhere to be a magical amount of time—reviewing my writing projects, what I was hoping to get, my goals and aspirations, and all around living a happy and joyous life. I had a small card in my wallet that I used as a cheat sheet. I kept it up to date, and within a couple of months I needed to rewrite it, because everything began singing for me.

That's when I began getting many freelance jobs with magazines, agencies, and companies. Some of them paid super well. And most of the projects I loved. Stories about artists, inventors, super athletes, reformed drunk drivers, a nudist camp, secret tunnels, sunken ferries, a gigolo, a guy who thought he was Houdini wrapped in twelve feet of chain and twenty-one padlocks jumping into the Mississippi, the Roller Derby, blackjack, horse racing, walking on coals, and the guy who owned the Harlem Globetrotters.

Soon that positive expectancy became a way of life for me, and I began invoking what I now call the Law of Attraction automatically. But instead of ask, believe, receive, it is for me imagine, desire, believe, and act, and all infused with powerful doses and intense feelings of happiness, joy, peace, contentment, and gratefulness.

I have fun with it, too. When I was purchasing my beautiful peroba wood bed, I had an obstinate, unbending, bullheaded, intractable saleslady who would not budge from her Pedestal of Price. So, I looked at her and firmly spoke in my most Charlton Heston part-the-Red-Sea voice, "I invoke the Law of Attraction. I ask for a substantial discount. I believe I will receive a substantial discount. And I graciously receive a substantial discount." I put out both arms, quaking slightly, because she was built like a refrigerator and could easily do me in. (She was built more like a brick shithouse, but I don't want to be disrespectful.)

She rolled her eyes, turned, and walked away.

"Hey," I said, "I am just trying to break you."

She stopped. Without looking back, she said, "You did. I'll throw in the dresser at a seventy percent discount. But the bed is at full price."

"And one nightstand?"

She turned to me. "One? Are you single?"

"Yes, but I already have one, and I don't want to be single forever, so I need the second one. The Universe needs to see I'm serious."

"That's good Feng Shui," she said. "Follow me."

Come to think of it, the Universe did provide us the Butterscotch Clipper, so the Law of Attraction works.

By the way, dear reader, have you invoked the Law of Attraction to find the treasure yourself? If not, maybe you can borrow Lane's *Living the Law of Attraction* Paraliminal. That Paraliminal was created by Jack Canfield, who was a star in *The Secret*—he's the king of the Law of Attraction, and Paul Scheele, who invented the Paraliminals in the first place.

Lane has asked me to "invoke the Law," as he calls it, many times. Once, the cleaners crushed the buttons on the sleeve of two of his dark shirts. They replaced the buttons free of charge, but used white thread instead of black thread. "They stood out like white stripes on a zebra," as Lane tells the story.

The cleaners said they replace buttons with a sewing machine that only has white thread. No amount of logic could get them to buck up and replace the buttons with black thread. So Lane said, "I will ask you one more time to make me whole and replace the buttons with black threads, or I will bring my friend over who will invoke the Law of Attraction."

The clerk firmly held her ground. "Bring him on."

"I'll be back in thirty minutes."

As it happens I was heading over to Lane's apartment, and in about a half hour we walked through the launderer's doors. Silence overtook the space. The clerk walked to the front counter, planting both fists on the counter. The other workers put their stuff down and walked to the front, flanking the clerk.

Lane and I stood still, eyes darting, wondering *what the heck?*

Then I noticed the uncanny resemblance between the clerk

and the saleslady at the furniture gallery. They had to be siblings. It obviously was show time.

I stepped forward and channeled Charlton Heston once
again. The hanging shirts absorbed a lot of the dramatics of
the voice, but it was still pretty darn good. "I invoke the Law
of Attraction. I ask for buttons sewn on Lane's shirt with black
thread. I believe I will receive buttons sewn with black thread.
And I graciously receive buttons sewn with black thread." She
nodded. "Come back tomorrow for your shirts." The others
turned and went back to their jobs. Lane stood there completely amazed. I smiled, but he did not see my smile, nor did he see
her wink. I never fessed up, until writing these words (Sorry
Lane!).

One thing is for sure, both Lane and the Ladies of the
Launderers had stories to tell. I'm sure the gals were on the
floor rolling when we left.

21

A Streak of White Lace

WE ALL TOOK A CYCLING, kayaking, and hiking "active vacation" to New Zealand three years ago with a few other friends including Marty, who, we learned two weeks before the trip, had never ridden a bicycle. Ever.

"Aren't you concerned?" I asked.

"No. How difficult can it be? I see old people and kids riding bikes everywhere."

"But, Marty, it takes balance and some skill. You need to learn how."

"I'll be fine. I'll figure it out when I'm there. I'm thirty-eight years old and should be able to ride a bike."

I couldn't believe he was spending almost seventy-five hundred dollars on a cycling vacation halfway around the world to not bicycle. Plus, while the rest of us were on machines getting into better shape, Marty was oblivious to any need to ready his body. He spent his spare time reading about *The Lord of the Rings* sites in New Zealand.

"About tomorrow," Marty told our guide on the eve of our first ride. She had never had a guest on a cycling trip in the fifteen years of running tours who had never been on a bike, but she was ready for the challenge. After we all took off on our bikes, our guide helped Marty onto a bicycle. He rode twenty feet, not in a straight line, not quite upright, and vowed he'd never ride again other than in the vans. She agreed with him. While we were pedaling about, Marty gallivanted off on side *Lord of the Rings* tours.

After three cycling days of sore butts, I tried wearing two pairs of cycling shorts. Two pairs of gel pads had to be better than one, especially for my bony butt. It worked so well that everyone was doubling up on the fifth day, even though the double-gels made us all look like we were wearing diapers. Filled diapers at that.

The trip taught us the value of high-quality bicycles. Riding was so easy. Our bodies, other than our butts, were not sore. We were wiped every day, but feeling great. The wine and beer helped, as you would guess. So, when Tom called around for bicycle rentals for today's ride, he made sure we were fit with titanium road bikes. The route he had selected was an out and back, but QB Earl, Sue, and Lane only felt like doing the eleven miles out, so Tom arranged for the Butterscotch Clipper to be waiting for us at the end replete with comfort, food, and booze.

About a mile into the ride Sue was thinking twice about the stack of pancakes and pile of bacon she had for breakfast. "I'm on holiday," she had said when she ordered. "Of course, I may as well just smear them on my hips, and cut out the middle man, if it didn't taste soooo good."

Tom, Lane, and I each had a bowl of chopped spinach, covered with steel cut oatmeal, and topped with sliced strawberries. The waitress had a hard time writing down our order, but got it perfectly right, and we were loving the ride.

QB Earl was content with three poached eggs, drizzled with olive oil and green pepper sauce, not even paying attention to the rest of us.

Lane made sure we had plenty of chocolate for energy, not that we needed it for eleven miles.

When my friend Robert ran the Polar Race to the North Pole, he ate a gallon-sized ziplock bag of fifty frozen broken-up Snickers bars every day as snacks between meals just to the get the calories he needed. It was a gruesome race—four hundred miles on foot, dragging a 100-pound sled at minus forty degrees while dodging polar bears. He finished it in seventeen days, twenty hours, forty-three minutes, and fifty-one seconds, at the age of sixty!

He needed chocolate for survival. We needed it for... for... for good taste.

The scenery wasn't as beautiful as New Zealand, but the cadence of the pedaling lulled us into tranquility. It wasn't until New Zealand did I first experience that tranquility. The scenery got us there, but it was the well-designed bikes and proper pedaling that kept us in the flow.

Proper pedaling? That's what I asked when our guide brought it up. She had three huge tips. Try them out for yourself. You'll never go back.

First, keep your hip, knee, and ankle lined up. In other words, don't let your knee wobble in and out.

Second, about your pedal form. When pedaling, come over the top of your stroke with your toes pointed down. Then level out, and drop your heel. "Like you're scraping dog poop from your shoe," said our guide. And then as you go up, get the foot out of the way of the pedal so it doesn't slow down the bike.

Third, cadence. It is most efficient to maintain a cadence somewhere between sixty and ninety strokes a minute. "Shift as often as you need to keep the cadence," she said. I had thought changing the cadence would be better, but she gracefully put me in my place.

We pow-wowed before today's ride to remind each other of proper pedaling and two rules: 1) ride single file to make it less likely to be thrown by a car, and 2) go at your own pace. Don't worry about the others. Do what feels best for your body and we'll meet up at the Butterscotch Clipper. About now, Tom is way out in front, Lane and I are together, and Sue and QB Earl are somewhere behind us.

Lane and I caught up with Tom at about nine miles, at the entrance to a state park. He was sitting in the shade, leaning up against a tree. Lane wasted no time getting off his bike and pulling out chocolate. The three of us sat there enjoying the breeze until Sue and QB Earl caught up. We agreed that champagne was in order, but since we were on bikes, we settled for water and chocolate.

Off we went for the final two miles, sticking together as a peloton. Tom didn't speed ahead and Sue and QB Earl kept up with Lane and me, lagging a bit. Life is good.

A titch down a side road a streak of white lace was bearing down, not stopping at the intersection, swooping past us, standing up to pedal harder. My Gawd, she looked like Quarry Girl. Same ginger hair. But what is she doing wearing lace and streaking through a park on a bicycle? Where we are?

"Hey, that's Quarry Girl." I pulled over. Everyone stopped.

"Wasn't that Quarry Girl?"

"No," said Sue, "She wouldn't be here."

"Though the dress was beautiful," said Lane, "but completely inappropriate."

"Wait, are you nuts? That was her," I said.

"I don't think so," said Tom, "but let's pedal to catch up."

We jumped back on our bikes. She was quite a way down the road already. I figured we could catch up, because we had pedal power. She stood up to get power, which is a waste of energy, so with our form, we should catch up (if only our New Zealand guide could hear me now!). But that cyclist had enough energy to cobble dogs, being younger than us.

Tom, Lane, and I took off fast. Adrenaline works. Sue and QB Earl lagged. I could feel the large muscles on the back of my legs work. And the hamstrings. It felt good. We were closing the gap. She was back to sitting in the saddle. As we got closer it certainly looked more and more like Quarry Girl, from the back anyway.

But wait, she had a bamboo flute slung over her shoulder. It was Quarry Girl.

"Hey," I shouted, pedaling harder. Tom and Lane joined the shouts. She looked back slightly, swinging out her right arm, motioning us to catch up.

"Pull over," I shouted. She just waved more and pedaled.

When we got caught up, she said, "I'm late for a wedding. I can't stop."

Wedding? What the heck.

"Okay. Enjoy!" I shouted.

"No, come along," she yelled back. "You'll have fun."

I looked to Tom. He nodded. Lane eagerly seconded it. So we followed along, our pace slowing a bit, veering right on another side road. The trees were gorgeous, wonderful fragrances from the woods, but what was she doing here? A wedding? How weird. We can't crash a wedding. But considering all of Tom's stories of crashing weddings in his 20s, why not. But there are five of us. Her hair was flowing. Her dress was flowing. I pulled out my phone to grab a photo. It's just too much.

I looked to Lane. He wore a huge smile, nodding like a kid chasing the ice cream truck. Tom kept focused ahead. I couldn't tell where Sue and QB Earl were, because I don't like looking back when pedaling. I hope they caught our turn.

As we approached a parking area, the Butterscotch Clipper came into view. This is the end of our ride? And there's a wedding? It should be feeling a little creepy, I thought, but I was actually feeling light and joyous. This is story-worthy cool.

Quarry Girl bounced off the road and pedaled into the woods. There's a path. We followed. Slowly, because it wasn't wide. Branches hit me. I love nature. I can't believe how many people live in the city and never get out to enjoy this. Chasing a strange girl through the woods to a wedding with people we don't even know. Lane behind me, Tom staying back to wait for Sue and QB Earl.

She can't be after the treasure. Can she? The wedding would explain why we kept running into her. A series of explainable coincidences. There's a clearing ahead. Water. It's the river. A half dozen people are standing looking at the river. All dressed similar to Quarry Girl, except the guys, but their clothes are light and breezy, too. It has to be a wedding.

Quarry Girl laid her bicycle down and ran over to the group. "I'm sorry. I'm late. And I brought friends I ran into." She turned and gestured to Lane and me just like the old man gestured to the Butterscotch Clipper, as if introducing her favorite people in the world.

Tom arrived seconds later with Sue and QB Earl, dropping their bikes, joining the crowd. The wedding folks greeted all of us with open and welcoming arms. One brought over a basket of wildflowers, giving us each a mini-bouquet, slipping a daisy into Sue's hair. And the video guy was filming everything.

"It's as if you were expecting us," I said smiling, feeling happy and grateful for the wonderful experience.

The guy who seemed to be the groom opened his arms to me with a warm hug. "We thought it would just be our close friends," he said, "but new friends showed. Here in the middle of nowhere. I'll remember this day forever."

As if weird could get weirder, we were all mingling as old friends. They poured glasses of sparkling pomegranate juice, sparkling with champagne, that is. How refreshing. Of course, we looked meaningfully into each other eyes as we toasted ourselves, the day, the happy couple, and the beautiful experiences of life. I could see love in their eyes, and in my friends. Everyone's eyes were wet. Sue and Lane were moments away from bawling. The bride had beat them, crying and crying.

The most official-looking guy asked, "Perhaps we can commence with the ceremony?" Spontaneously we all raised our glasses, walked to the water's edge, and witnessed a beautiful exchange of vows, with Quarry Girl—I mean Marie—playing her beaded bamboo flute. We had finally learned her name from one of the wedding party.

"All we have in life is the moment we are in right now," said the minister. "The past is all gone, memories in a book we can open or close whenever we'd like. Memories we can carry with us or freely release.

"The future is yet to come. It can hold our hopes and

dreams, our castles in the air, but they do not exist, they cannot exist, because all that exists, exists only in the moment we are in right now.

"At any moment we can choose what to feel, and that is our life. The best moments are when we feel happy, joyous, at peace, content, and grateful all at once. These emotions provide full balance in our lives, aligning us with the five elements of the universe—wood, fire, earth, metal, and water."

Quarry Girl Marie playing along, her music floating with his words.

"They give us our purpose. To live happy, joyous, at peace, content, and grateful in every moment. That's love. That's the expression of the universe, the radiance of God."

We all smiled. I could feel tingling through my body. Every cell was alive, and it seemed everyone was with me.

"It is right now we come together in love as Peter and Ruth come together in love. We celebrate our lives, we bless our love, and we witness how we are all one."

As the minister pronounced them husband and wife, I knew this was the golden ring Quarry Girl sang about, and we all began dancing as pixies, an ecstatic waltz of free-form movements, completely lost in time.

Soon we were sitting on blankets laughing, and crying, and eating a raw food feast that began with hummus, guacamole, and flax crackers. Then a sweet spinach salad with oranges, red onion, strawberries, sunflower seeds, pecans, and cherry vinaigrette. And a pesto pasta made with zucchini noodles, tomatoes, peppers, marinated mushrooms, and walnuts.

Sometime later I said, "Well, we probably should be moving on and leaving you all to yourselves. We intruded on your celebration, which we all thoroughly enjoyed, and it's time for you to enjoy each other."

"No way," said one of the gals. "Let's play duck, duck, goose." And that began a string of games that led through the afternoon and into the evening.

"Let's all of us go back to the Butterscotch Clipper, and I'll fix dinner," said Sue. "I think we have enough food to keep the party going. We can dip into tomorrow's stash. There's enough."

"And I'll mix up cosmos," said QB Earl.

With that, Tom called the bicycle rental company, and we tidied up the grounds and made our way to the Butterscotch Clipper, where we celebrated into the night with our new friends.

22

Hodaddy Tsktsk

"MAYBE WE WERE ALL FRIENDS in a past circle of life," said Sue the next morning. "I'm sure Oprah would have agreed if she were still on air."

"It is just so weird that we kept running into her," I said.

"What's wrong with weirdness?" asked Lane matter-of-factly.

"Or maybe it's just a strange string of coincidences to bring us all together," said Tom.

"But we won't be seeing them again, and I don't even know where they're from. We can't even invite them for dinner some-time," I said.

"But maybe we'll see them again," smiled Lane. "We can share information then."

"You know what I mean."

"But why can't every moment be a beautiful experience, just like the minister man said," said Sue. "'At any moment we can choose what to feel, and that is our life.' Who cares if it doesn't fit with anything else in our life. I really enjoyed yesterday, and we'll no doubt talk about it forever."

Tom jumped in, "I know I will."

"Me too," said QB Earl.

"Did anyone else notice that in the entire time we were together there were no undertones of jealousy, anger, blame, worry, pessimism?" asked Sue. "No one complained of anything. No one expressed any disappointment about any area of their lives. There's something magical happening."

"Everything was so light and expansive," said Tom.

"Are we concerned they may be looking for the treasure, too?" I asked.

"Spoke too soon," said Tom.

"Worry just reared its ugly head," laughed Sue.

"No, I'm serious," I said.

"They just had a wedding. That explained everything," said Tom.

"Does it really?"

"What?" asked Sue. "Did you think the wedding was a ruse just to get to know us? Did anyone ask about a treasure hunt? Or where we would be going tomorrow? We didn't bring it up. I don't think any of them tried to sneak it out of us."

Everyone shook their heads.

"Not me," I said.

"So, there. It was just a nice diversion in our quest for the gold," smiled Sue.

I simply gazed at her. Hard to disagree. The blue sapphires in her hair glistened in the lights. I was so happy she was in my life. What a gem. I started to wonder where this competitive streak in me came from. Who cares if they are looking for the treasure. It's a game. I should really be accepting and easygoing about it. Instead of being so closed, maybe I should listen to that spiritual teacher Jeddah Mali and reach out. Like what I learned from her *Seeds of Enlightenment* course:

> If our society is going to evolve, if we are going to experience life as expansive instead of contracting all of the time, we need to change how we relate to people.
>
> Instead of being so competitive, we need to be more tolerant of each other, even reaching into being cooperative, maybe even co-creative, for if you truly understand who you are, you would know we are all interconnected.
>
> There is no reason at all for all of the competitiveness in our lives. When you are playing the game of football, fine, but the game of life?

We all moved slowly that morning, chatting away, enjoying tea and coffee, blueberries and raspberries, and raw almonds. Yet, I really wanted to get cracking and on the road. *Hup! Hup! Today's the day to find the treasure!* But the others wanted to relax. "Let's not rush. There's plenty of time." Sue and Tom went out for a run, so the rest of us practiced qigong in the morning sun, the temperature in the low 70s. Nothing could be finer, except for the shower in the Butterscotch Clipper.

Even now, I marvel at the perfect sizing of that amazingly compact shower, sink, and toilet assembly. Whoever designed it must certainly have won an award. It felt spacious and not cramped. That convinced me that RV living could be in my future. It was thirty-nine billion times better than the shower in the beast, where half the time the shower curtain stuck to my butt.

I told everyone we were a mere fifty-five miles from the treasure, and I asked if anyone had figured it out. Lane said, "Of all of the clues, 'Hodaddy tsktsk prettify introfly South Georgia' was the most revealing."

"What?" Sue, QB Earl, and Tom sang in unison.

"How could that tell you anything?" asked Sue. "Hodaddy tsk-what? Pretty Woman apple pie?"

"I just loved how the words felt in my mouth. I kept saying them over and over and over and over," said Lane.

"Hodaddy what?" asked Sue.

Lane coaxed, "Tsktsk."

Sue uttered, "Hodaddy tsktsk," leaving room for Lane to continue with "prettify introfly."

"Apple pie," said Sue.

"No, South Georgia," said Lane.

Then the others joined in, "Hodaddy tsktsk prettify introfly South Georgia," with Lane helping out, them repeating it over and over, dropping off "South Georgia," "Hodaddy tsktsk prettify introfly, hodaddy tsktsk prettify introfly, hodaddy tsktsk prettify introfly, hodaddy tsktsk prettify introfly."

Tom asked, "Does dropping off 'South Georgia' matter?"

"I'd prefer apple pie," said Sue. "Or peach pie!"

"Beats me," said Lane, ignoring Sue. "It just sounds better. Although I do love Savannah."

"That's east Georgia," said Tom.

"This clue stopped me completely," said Sue, reading "Et4ue2I2l6jA2t4ulB15ys5oj."

"Ah!" exclaimed Lane. "Me, too. I had a cross word and nasty thought when I saw it. A string of them. I didn't know whether it was a puzzle or whether you needed a cypher."

"I don't even know what a cypher is," said QB Earl.

"I stared at it for hours. Nothing came to me," added Lane.

"Well?" I asked. Everyone looked at me. "Where are we going?"

Lane gave an answer, very assuredly, no doubt, and he was spot on. I smiled. Everyone looked around. They smiled. Of course, given where we were, it would have been a fair guess. Still QB Earl asked, "How the hell did you get that from 'hodaddy tsktsk pretty pie apple pie?'"

"I was chanting it to myself in the shower and it just streaked into my mind. I wrote it on the shower door in the steam, and there it was staring at me, not like that other one you just read," said Lane, turning to Sue. "Et4ue2I2l6jA2t4ulB15ys5oj."

"And, we still have to decipher that little poem, because I haven't figured that out," I said. They knew what I was talking about, because it was in the stack of clues. "Just maybe it will become clear as we get near."

Sue read it aloud.

> *You wouldn't guess by looking at a tree,*
> *That it could eat anything other than sunshine.*
>
> *but as the sun shines down*
> *just north of this old town*
> *the eyes they look ahead*
> *its mouth it opens wide*
> *in darkness lips curl over*
> *the boulder it freely eats*
>
> *You wouldn't guess by looking at a tree,*
> *That it could eat anything other than sunshine.*

Everyone froze in silence, not having the foggiest idea what it meant. Then, as if a video was taken off pause, we all agreed it seemed interesting, eagerly readied ourselves for the final drive, and chatted more about where they had gotten on their own trying to solve the puzzles and clues. They all had different takes, and everyone was so close. Perhaps had it not been so self-evident to me when I first saw it, we would have figured it out together. I guess I can be co-creative. And I guess that's why I still thought Quarry Girl, Marie, could be on the hunt—it was so obvious to me.

Perhaps she knew how to find the treasure once she got to the location, but perhaps she didn't know the final location. We're close enough that she could guess where we'd be heading, but how did she get this far along? And the wedding? How could the wedding even be? If she were on the hunt, the wedding doesn't make sense. I think it was just chance. She's not on the hunt.

Within an hour the Butterscotch Clipper transported us to the 1920s for an amazing lunch in a classy old bar that would have been more amazing had we not been chomping to find the treasure. Finally Lane picked up the tab, something he is not prone to do, and said, "Let's go get the pot. I can't take it anymore."

Of course, he didn't want to say, "Let's go get the treasure," in case someone in the place knew about the treasure hunt, but his saying, "Let's go get the pot" as in "pot of gold" still got others in the joint to turn heads.

"Not that kind of pot," said Sue, semi-scolding those at the next table who just smiled. "Crockpot. We're going to a Rock the Crock crockpot party, and we need to find our crockpot."

"Come on. Let's go," I said, tugging at Sue's arm. I turned

to the table and mouthed, "She's a crackpot."

"I heard that," she said.

As we walked out of the place, QB Earl said, "I've been trying to figure out what to call us."

"What was that?" asked Tom.

"You know. Dynamic Duo, Three Musketeers or Three Stooges, Fantastic Four, The Magnificent Seven. There is nothing for five of us. What could we call ourselves?" he asked.

"Five gold rings," said Sue.

"The Potheads," said Lane.

"We need a number," said QB Earl.

"The Potheads Five," said Lane.

"Where is this coming from?" Tom asked QB Earl.

"I'm just feeling we're on a mission, and we should have a name."

Seeing the Butterscotch Clipper down the street, "How about the Butterscotch Five?" I asked.

"That's it," said Sue. "The Butterscotch Five."

"The Butterscotch Five," we all bellowed at full throttle, raising our right hands as if we had drinks.

As you understand by now, our natural inclination was to get a cocktail, but we had agreed that today would be booze-free until after we found the treasure.

23

%@&$$!*#

When the others pressed Lane for how he knew exactly where next to park the Butterscotch Clipper, he rapped, "Nadatrace, nadasoda, nadacurl, nadacocoa, beenbitt."

"Ha!" belted Tom. "White boy can't rap."

"Oh, Tommy, stop that," Sue said, pushing Tom along into the Clipper. "You can't either."

"Sure can," said Tom. "Lane, give me the cheat sheet." He grabbed the clue card from Lane. "Nadatrace, nadasoda, nadacurl, nadacocoa, beenbitt."

"Told you so! Told you so!" laughed Sue.

"How'd you figure that out?" asked QB Earl to Lane.

"I applied the same logic to that clue I had to 'hodaddy tsktsk prettify introfly South Georgia,'" he said. "Or near the same. Or maybe the reverse. I don't know. It was nadaeasy, but I got it anyway."

"Okay smartypants," said QB Earl, "How do we get there?"

Lane pulled out his phone, tapped the map app, and pointed, "That-a-way."

"I agree," I assured the others.

As we pulled out on our final ride, Tom played the epic and bombastic album *1492: Conquest of Paradise*, which mirrored our journey and set the mood for our final trek. Gloriously ethereal, super serious (or, super mission driven), and, yes, somewhat over the top, the music filled every cubic inch of the Butterscotch Clipper, causing the pounded copper wall at the back end to vibrate. Life is good.

When we landed, off trekked the Butterscotch Five with me in the lead and Lane chanting, "O-Ee-Yah! Eoh-Ah! O-Ee-Yah! Eoh-Ah!" The others joined in like the castle guards for the Wicked Witch of the West. "O-Ee-Yah! Eoh-Ah! O-Ee-Yah! Eoh-Ah!"

Tom wove in his own version, "O-Re-O by Nabi-Sco! O-Re-O by Nabi-Sco!" The perfect follow to the *Conquest of Paradise*.

Somewhat later, after our rolling inanity gave way to serious hiking, I said, "Here it is."

They looked at me, somewhat agog.

"Sue, read it again," I said.

You wouldn't guess by looking at a tree,
That it could eat anything other than sunshine.

but as the sun shines down
just west of this old town
the eyes they look ahead
its mouth it opens wide

in darkness lips curl over
the boulder it freely eats

You wouldn't guess by looking at a tree,
That it could eat anything other than sunshine.

"Now that's funny," said Sue.

"Perfectly funny," said QB Earl.

"Cool. Does that mean the treasure is here?" asked Lane.

"Nope," I said. "It's a marker. From here we count off eight hundred and forty paces."

"How about a picture, first?" asked Sue.

"Great idea," said Tom. "This is too fun." Which, of course, made us all think about how wonderful a glass of wine would be, but off we went. Eight hundred and forty paces, with Lane counting. We were on a mission.

"Now what?" asked QB Earl when Lane hit 840.

"Simple," I said, beaming a wide smile, "We follow the direction of the Scarecrow." I threw my arms in the air, swinging every direction, pretending I was the brain-free scarecrow, and off we went down our own yellow brick road. I half expected the group to be singing "Follow the Yellow Brick Road," but not a peep out of anyone. If we had speakers with us, Tom would be playing *Conquest of Paradise* again.

I was getting more excited for the treasure by the step, because I knew we were so close, and when we walked over a wide rock formation clearly in our path, my heart jumped up a beat. "Lane, get a-counting. We have one hundred and ninety paces to go," I said, hoping no one had yet found the treasure.

I had been saying all along it wasn't the prize money, but I've been thinking more and more about that fifty grand. We were going to party. Maybe a vacation to Maui, or Paris, if we could get the Butterscotch Clipper to fly. Yes, there was the joy of the hunt, the thrill of figuring it out, the delight of the Butterscotch Five, but the idea of fifty thousand dollar-coins was magnetic. Then… Quarry Girl passed through my head. She wasn't there. We were by ourselves. But there she was in my head, and I quickened the pace. The sun streamed on us, but thanks to Lane and his slathering sunblock, our pod was protected. We kinda moved like a pod. We were pretty darn close together. The ground was dappled in wildflowers of yellow, white, red, and lavender, like daytime lightning bugs stealing our attention now and then, providing texture to our walk, making sure we saw living joy.

"… one eighty-five, one eighty-six, one eighty-seven, one eighty-eight, one eighty-nine, one ninety." Lane stopped counting. We stopped walking. We turned left. A beautiful and big rock formation lay straight ahead. I raced to it, ducking to go under some low-hanging, head-scratching branches, feeling exhilarated, stopping at the end of what was a ledge that dropped off quite a bit. The treasure would be right below it. But what?! Quarry Girl. On the left. Climbing up the hill. Did she see me? She was running up the hill. Yes, she did. She's after the treasure.

I turned back, almost pushing Sue over the mini-cliff, not knowing what the heck was going on, needing to be goat-footed and find a way down and around the ledge, through a rock narrows, and…

Quarry Girl and I both stopped four feet from the treasure, four feet from each other. Like a golden triangle.

I looked at her, completely speechless, thoughtless, emotions all over the place.

She said one word, a word I was not expecting, a word that

would freeze my brain.

"Dad."

I didn't move. Nothing registered.

"Dad," she said again. Her eyes glistened.

I didn't move. No registration. I hadn't even seen her friends from the wedding come from around the rocks.

"It's me. Judy."

I felt tingling in my head. My eyes welled.

I looked up to look at my friends, but they were already down from the ledge, behind me. Sue, Lane, QB Earl, and Tom. I was about to break out bawling. Of course, Sue had beaten me to it. She was full out crying. As soon as our eyes connected, she heaved audible sobs. The others had Grand Canyon-huge smiles.

"Hug her," said Lane. "Hug her."

I turned and opened my arms as she fell into me. I held her tight, crying into her ginger hair, the pent up love of three decades pouring from my heart.

When Judy and I finally released our embrace, I turned to the others, immediately bawling again, "You knew. You all knew. You toads knew." That's when I noticed Tom's partner, Paul. "You knew," I said pointing to him. "I wondered why you didn't join us. Unexpected work trip, darn you. You were behind this. All of you. And there wasn't a treasure hunt?"

"For you," said QB Earl.

"You guys made this all up?" I turned to Lane. "I thought that poem about the rock-eating tree sounded an awful lot like you."

"We'll tell you all about it," said Sue. "First, where is that champagne?" And within seconds the first of four bottles popped open.

"No, no, no, no," I said. "How did this begin? How did you meet each other and put two and two together?"

"Bali," said Tom.

"Bali?" I asked.

Tom smiled. "Ahhhh," I said, "the gal playing the flute!"

"We'll tell you the whole story, but first, let's introduce the wedding party from a slightly different perspective," Paul said.

"So the wedding was a hoax?" I asked.

"Of course," smiled Lane.

"These are my best friends in the world," said Judy Marie, our Quarry Girl, my daughter.

After the reintroductions we sat on blankets, the same ones from the wedding, and ate cherries, strawberries, and dark chocolate.

"Tell me about Bali," I smiled. "And who the heck carried all of this champagne this far?"

24

My Froggy

Tom watched the sun rise over the Badung Strait while everyone else slept. He loved the mornings, getting out of bed as soon as he became conscious of himself as a human being. While others would roll over for more sleep, Tom would engage with the day.

This morning he headed beachside, a short stroll from his villa, drawn by the enchanting sounds of a Balinese bamboo flute, ocean waves, and morning birds. A gal with a frangipani flower in her ginger hair, beads flowing around her neck, and a wispy lacy gown played surreal music. He sat lost in the moment, getting up only when he realized she hadn't been playing for a while.

"Good morning," greeted Tom. She smiled. "That's beautiful. Thank you."

"You don't sound Aussie," she said.

"Say again?"

"It seems every American-looking person is from Australia, and you don't sound Australian."

"Nope. From the States. Staying here for a couple of weeks."

Both were on vacation, she staying in a motel a half mile inland, and as Miss Fortuna would have it, they lived just a few miles from each other back home. Tom recalled a monthlong trip to Europe during college to take a course called "Culture and Skiing in Europe." While gazing up at the beautiful and historical church of Mondsee in Austria, he began talking to the gal standing next to him. Soon he realized she was speaking English, and he turned to her. He recognized a patch on her stocking cap from a place not too far from home, and then he said, "Janny?"

She looked at him.

"Tom?"

They grew up next door to each other in Babbitt. She, too, was a Babbitt Rabbit. *Babbitt Rabbits hats off to thee. To thy cottontails hopping will ever be. Hoppy bopping to victory, raw, raw, raw for bunny power, hippity, hoppity, hippity, hoppity, hats off to the Babbitt Rabbits.*

Key change, up a notch. *We're the jack rabbits and off we get, eating lettuce, carrots, and other grits, hopping, bopping to victory, raw, raw, raw, for bunny power, hippity, hoppity, hippity, hoppity, hats off to the Babbitt Rabbits. B-A-B-B-I-T-T R-A-B-B-I-T-S Babbitt Rabbits, Raw!*

While running into someone in Bali who lives a couple of towns over from him wasn't exactly the same as running into his neighbor in Austria, it kept the conversation going as they wandered thirty minutes down the beach and back. By then Tom's friends were awake, the cooks had arrived, and, kitchen clanging, they all made it to the beach.

"Would you like to join us for coffee and breakfast?" Tom asked.

"Do you have tea?" she asked.

"Of course."

"Of course."

The morning featured banana French toast, fresh fruit, plenty of coffee and tea, and full-on laughter with Tom's friends, taking them well into gin and tonic time, which was always the same time every day: as soon as breakfast was finished.

She loved the story of the frogs and Tom's Frogyrinth. When she met the frogs at their Bali beach compound, she was completely taken. She asked Tom to snap pictures of her by each frog, including the one playing the Balinese flute.

"You have to invite me to the Frogyrinth when it is ready," she said.

"Will you bring your beautiful flute?" asked Tom.

"Of course! I'll even wear this dress," she said twirling around. "I found this in a shop just up the street from here."

"Deal," he said. "Where did you get the flute?"

"I've been playing flutes for years, but I got this one here."

"Gorgeous," he said. "You found it beaded?"

"Oh, no, I did that," she smiled, running her fingers along the river of beads on the back of the flute.

"What's the story of the stone turtle?" Tom asked.

"That was a mistake," she laughed. "It's a relationship turtle, thinking it might bring me a partner some day." She kept laughing. Tom smiled, but without getting the joke. "Only after I finished beading did I realize I needed two turtles for a relationship. I had one! That wouldn't work! I went back to the bead shop and they didn't have any more. So, it's a single relationship turtle." Tom laughed and laughed with her.

"But I think the turtle is a symbol of protection," said Tom. "The shell protects you. It is a totem for you."

"Perhaps," she laughed. "But it looks more like a cell for my heart. Forever encased in a turtle shell."

Tom rolled his eyes. She laughed more. "I'm really okay with everything. I'm just having fun."

A year later, just after Tom took delivery of the frogs, he sorted through the hundreds of photos he took of the Bali trip. He wasn't one for organizing photos in a timely manner, but since the frogs were on his mind he took time to revisit the vacation.

He loved the photos of his new ginger friend with the frogs in Bali, enjoying her lighthearted playfulness, and the simple beauty of her expressions. There was something very familiar about her, and he found himself pulled to the photos again and again over the next couple of weeks.

Sorting through photos became a good winter project for Tom, and one day when he was flipping through an album of photos from a party at my house, he stopped and studied my eyes at length. He had looked into my eyes many times over the years. Good friends do, especially when toasting. But this time he was seeing something else—the waves of Bali, the sparkle of his new friend Judy. He flipped from one photo to the next. He pulled up photos of Judy.

Those were the same eyes. The noses were similar. And the lips. Thin. The mouths. Small.

"I immediately called you, Nels," Tom told me. "But you were away on some writing assignment and didn't answer your phone. I figured you had to be related somehow, because the similarities were so uncanny. So I called Judy. It took me a while to find her number. I hadn't spoken with her since Bali. I asked her to lunch the next day, loaded photos on my iPad, and...well..."

"What did you think when he told you about the photos?" I asked.

"He didn't tell me. At lunch he whipped out his iPad and showed me photos of his friend. I wasn't impressed at first, because a lot of people look like a lot of people, but when he put our photos side by side, I thought, 'This is weird.'"

"How did you know...," I began to ask.

"That's the cool part. I didn't," said Tom.

"Me neither," said Judy.

"It was furthest from either of our minds. I didn't even know that Judy didn't know her father."

"It wasn't until I asked Tom what you had said when he showed you the photos," said Judy.

"And I said, 'I haven't showed Nelson. He's out of town,'" said Tom.

"I froze. I didn't breathe. I recognized the name," she said. "My froggy."

"'You okay?' I asked her," said Tom.

"'Yes,' I said, shaking it off." Judy continued, "I needed time to think. I changed the subject. And that didn't do it. I was so distracted. I just had to get out of there. I made up some excuse and bolted."

"That was a little weird," said Tom, "but I always thought she was a little weird, so what the heck."

"My life was upside down, and I didn't know what to do about it. I so much wanted to meet my father, but what if he didn't want to meet me? You know. All of that stuff. I talked it over with my best girlfriend, and she convinced me to meet up with Tom again, and that's what the three of us did."

"I tell you, there was nothing further from my mind. I had no idea whatsoever," said Tom. "There was no connection at all. Not an inkling. As a matter of fact, after that initial lunch I had forgotten about the similarities. Thanksgiving was coming up, and my life was busy, but when we got together again and she told me about her frog named Nelson, it was my turn not to breathe. Before long I was smiling so huge. 'This is perfect! He so much wants to meet you.' I told her. 'He's talked about you forever.'"

"And the next thing you know, we're here," said Judy.

"But that was six months ago. Why didn't we just get together? How could you keep it from me? I'm thinking I should be mad at you," I said.

"That was the plan," laughed Tom. "But I called together Sue, Lane, and QB Earl, and the next thing we knew we were plotting, plotting, plotting."

"I should have known," I said.

"Hey," said Sue, "This was a once-in-a-lifetime opportunity to do something so cool, something beyond so cool, something we all will be talking about forever. Weren't you surprised? I know you were."

I started crying again. And Sue, Lane, QB Earl, Judy, and her friends joined. Bawling and sobbing. We were all so happy.

"But the treasure hunt? How the heck did you pull that off?"

25

Wily, Crafty, and Downright Clever

"I FOUND OUT ABOUT THE TREASURE HUNT at a meeting of The League of Uncommon Gentlemen," I said. "I found out about it on my own accord, you didn't even know about it, and I decided to go to the meeting on my own accord. You guys had nothing to do with that."

"Or did we?" asked Sue, somewhat coyly.

"How could you have?"

"How did you find out about the meeting?"

"From an ad."

"How did you find the ad?"

"I was reading an article in the neighborhood paper."

"How did you find out about the article?"

I couldn't immediately remember. "I was just flipping

through the newspaper," I said.

"Why?"

"I don't really remember. Other than it was in my apartment, and I picked it up."

"Do you subscribe to the paper?"

"No. I must have picked it up."

"Do you pick it up often?"

"Not really."

"You didn't this time," said Lane. "I dropped it off at your place."

"And I called you, telling you to read it," said QB Earl.

He did? I thought. After a half second, "That's right, you did. You called and said you had just read an interesting article about tea and bourbon and thought I would like it. And I did."

"Ever wonder why you liked it?" asked Lane.

"It was about bourbon and tea," I said.

"And?" asked Sue.

I didn't know what she was saying.

"It was about Buffalo Trace Bourbon and Fortnum & Mason tea," said Sue. "We knew you would love it, and we knew you could not *not* spend time reading it."

They all smiled at me.

"You wrote it?"

"We wrote it. And we wrote it to capture your attention to make sure you would spend time on the page and catch the ad."

Lane pulled out his mobile and began reading the article:

The Unlikely Marriage of Buffalo Trace Bourbon and Earl Grey Tea

A new drink appeared on the menu at the Red Brick Drinking Club, turning teetotalers tipsy with a blend of Buffalo Trace Bourbon and Earl Grey Tea from Fortnum & Mason.

Bartender Aaron Philress said, "I was drinking Earl Grey Tea in a glass coffee cup, looking at the golden color, which reminded me of my favorite bourbon for cocktails. I wondered how they would taste together, so I tried it. At first the mixture didn't taste right so I had to adjust proportions, and I found I really liked it. Especially with fresh lemon juice and a drop of honey."

He went on to say, "I brewed a pot of tea, iced it, and wrote up on the specials board, 'The Grey Buffalo—cocktail of Earl Grey Tea and Buffalo Trace Bourbon.' I knew I had a hit when patrons came back asking for it after I had removed it from the specials board."

It's become a hit with regulars including novelist Pete Bissonette who said, "It's become my signature drink, at least when I'm here at the Red Brick Drinking Club."

Novelist Jay Danler, author of the famous treasure hunt novel of the 1980s, *Kip's Armor*, said, "I'm now inspired to write a new novel." When asked why he hasn't written anything since then, he responded, "It could be that I hadn't yet discovered the special elixir of The Grey Buffalo, but in truth, my business took off leaving me little time to write. I'll for sure pick it up in the next circle of life."

Larson A. Herisp, president of The League of Uncommon Gentlemen, whose organization meets periodically at the Red Brick Drinking Club, said, "I tried it because of the special price and found its bright earthy flavor comforting. Now I even make it myself at home."

The Grey Buffalo is available every day. For the next week all proceeds from its sales will go to charity.

The Grey Buffalo

1 jigger of Buffalo Trace bourbon
1 jigger of Fortnum & Mason Earl Grey tea
Splash of freshly squeezed lemon
Drop of honey to taste

Mix honey into warm tea, combine ingredients in glass and stir. Serve with ice.

"How did you get the bartender to go for it?" I asked.
"I knew him," said Lane.
"No, he didn't," said Sue, "but after flashing his Persians, he knew him quite well."
We all smiled.
"And I knew the editor of the paper," said Tom. "She loved the article and agreed to give us an ad for The League of Uncommon Gentlemen at a special rate."
"But how did you know I would go to the meeting?"
"Come on," said Sue. "Buffalo Trace and tea?"
"And The League of Uncommon Gentlemen?" asked QB

Earl. "How could you resist that?"

"That perfect coincidence brought everything together," said Sue.

"That day I stopped over right after work," said Lane. "I brought the newspaper and left it on your table, and I brought up that novel you like so well with the murder. I must have said a thousand times, 'Those certainly were uncommon gentlemen in that club.'"

"I hadn't noticed you saying that."

"Did you notice when I asked 'Would you *go to the club* today if it were real?'" said Lane emphasizing "Go To The Club Today" as he spoke.

"Yah."

"I immediately said, 'I would *go to the club immediately*.'"

"You dog. You used embedded commands, hypnosis, and NLP on me. The same stuff from the Paraliminals."

"And it worked!"

"But how did you get me to sign up for the treasure hunt? That five thousand dollar entry fee was a lot of money."

"Easy," said Tom. "Do you remember the brochure for the treasure hunt? And how its design was nearly a duplicate of that novel's cover, the one about that social club?"

"Kinda."

"Doesn't matter. You were drawn to it. Hypnosis and NLP. You could not *not* be drawn to it. Plus it supported your favorite charity. And you had told me a month or so ago that you were going to up your contribution to them this year by five thousand, because of the super big writing gig you got."

"You are all dogs. You've manipulated me."

"We toyed with you," said Lane.

"There was no manipulation at all," said QB Earl.

"Ah, come on," said Sue. "Yes, there was. Full on manipulation. We worked our butts off to manipulate you."

"But how did you know I was going to take the bait and sign up for the treasure hunt?"

"Who called you that night?" asked Sue.

"You?" I asked.

"Yes, me. Do you remember why?"

"To manipulate me?"

"That's right," laughed Sue. "I called to get the recipe for the turkey burgers you had made that weekend, and I said, and I quote…" She paused, pulling out her phone and reading from it, "I really *find* our friendship is a *treasure*. Some people *hunt for gold* in all of the wrong places, when *it is right there in front of you*. I just want you to know I appreciate you, especially how you are always willing to take a risk, do something different, and include your friends. You're not one not to go for treasure. You are uncommon and you are always on the *hunt for new adventures*. Anyway, I gotta fly. Send me that recipe. And if you can think of anything fun to do this weekend, I'm game. Otherwise it will be a little boring."

"There you have it," I said.

"But how did you know that I would solve the treasure?" I asked.

One big collective eye roll.

"Am I that predictable?"

Another big collective eye roll.

"But those clues were difficult. I got lucky."

Another big collective eye roll.

"So you created the treasure hunt knowing I would be able to solve it immediately, but it would appear challenging for the average person?"

Big smiles.

"We collected the books you had read in the previous month and all of the writing assignments," said Tom. "And we crafted the clues from those."

"But how the heck did you find this location and tie it into the clues?"

Collective eye roll.

"You structured the clues and then figured out where they led?" I asked.

"How else," said Tom. "Otherwise we'd be at it for years."

"How did you get everything to happen on this weekend?"

"That's where we got a little duplicitous," said Sue. "I snuck a long peek at your calendar and figured out when you could take time away."

Lane added, "I also asked if we could go away that week."

"Then from that start date we worked backward. Making sure Judy and her friends could be mobilized, setting up the date of the beginning of the treasure hunt and the day the clues would arrive, and making sure we all got together that night to help you solve the treasure," said Tom.

"And if you couldn't do it—" said Sue, QB Earl interrupting with, "If you let us down—" back to Sue, "We would have solved it for you."

"One way or another we were going to be heading out this weekend."

"But why in the name of John the Baptist didn't you arrange for me to find a better RV than the beast?" I asked.

"Didn't think of it," said Lane.

"We just thought you could rent a decent RV at the last minute," said Tom.

"No idea we would be needing flea repellent," said Sue.

"You're forgiven," I laughed. "You did a great job with the Butterscotch Clipper. How did you sabotage the beast?"

"We had nothing to do with that," said Tom.

"Probably the Law of Attraction," said Lane.

"You found the Butterscotch Clipper all by yourself," said Sue. "The whole plan just had a massive kink in it when the beast wouldn't start, and we had no idea what would happen next, especially with the wedding coming up."

"The gods must be smiling. But how did you know our route? I kept it from you, giving you the opportunity to solve it on your own," I said.

"You toad," said Sue. "That added an interesting twist."

"And it made sure you didn't get suspicious," said Tom.

"But how did you arrange to get Judy to appear in the right places at the right time? Or the odd places and seemingly random times?"

"Ha!" said Paul. "Lots of bourbon." Everyone laughed and laughed.

"It was a bitch," said Tom.

"But luckily you made us solve the treasure on our own, because that way we could be on the Internet trying to map out what would happen in each city, and you would be none the wiser. Every chance we had we were plotting. You were on a treasure hunt, and we were plotting it as you went," said Sue.

"Here I thought you were on your phones and iPads all of the time trying to figure it out. I was so proud of you," I said.

"We were trying to figure it out!" said Tom. "Just not where the treasure was, but the adventure along the way."

"*Find A Friend* on our iPhones helped, too," said Lane.

"We were able to track you so we always knew where you were," said Paul.

"But I turned off my phone now and then," I said.

"But none of us did. We were all trackable by each other," said QB Earl.

"We were tracking everyone all of the time," said Paul, "and we were often just feet ahead of you."

"Do you remember when we climbed the tower, and you didn't want to go up?" asked Tom.

"I got you up there by talking about how beautiful it would be," said Sue. "I knew you would respond to beauty, but it was such an ugly tower, so I had to convince myself so I could convince you."

"But why climb the tower?" I asked.

"Because we needed to figure out spontaneously where we would hike next, and once we made the decision, we needed time for Judy, Paul, and the photographer to scout out a place for Judy to be playing," said Tom.

"If we had simply decided and then started walking, there is no way they could get out in front of us and set up. We needed the tower to slow you down!" said Sue.

"And we had to get the plan back to you guys," said Paul.

"And *Find A Friend* worked both ways," said Lane. "While you thought Tom was trying to solve the problem, he was watching Judy and Paul."

"Brilliant," I said.

"Thank you," everyone said in unison.

"Next question," I said, "Why Big Bob's Bar-B-Que?"

"That's the only place that would allow us to set up so Judy could perform," said Paul. "We visited a half-dozen restaurants."

"They all had excuses," said Judy. "'We don't do music.' 'We don't know you.' 'Our customers would be annoyed.' 'We don't have insurance for this.'"

"And on and on," said Paul. "We were almost ready to chuck the idea, when Big Bob said, 'Sure, why not. No free food, though.' And off we went."

"It makes sense, now," I said. "Tom, you cannot stand anything smoked."

"I know. I cringed. But what the heck."

"And it turned out quite delicious," said QB Earl, probably smelling the barbecue in his beard.

"I think I know why you changed the lyrics to the song," I said, looking to Judy.

"You caught that?" she asked.

"Caught what?" asked Sue.

"Judy played with the lyrics," said Tom.

Judy laughed.

"What?" asked Sue.

"I sang, 'As it goes along the ground, ground, ground till it leads you to the golden ring.'" said Judy.

"The lyrics are really, 'As it goes along the ground, ground, ground till it leads you to *the one you love*,'" said Tom.

"And that's me!" exclaimed Judy.

"Clever," said Sue. "You caught that, Nels?"

"When I was lying in bed after the incident with the police, I just couldn't fall asleep," I said. "So, I replayed the day and suddenly realized she changed the lyrics, and I thought it meant she was looking for the treasure."

"A twist," said Sue. "Cool."

"QB Earl, tell Nels about your temper tantrum," said Tom.

"That was fake, too?" I asked. "You're kidding."

"No. That was real. Kinda. Remember when my phone beeped and you picked it up to hand it to me?" said QB Earl.

"Okay, yup," I said.

"I saw a picture on it that Paul just sent me, and I had to get the phone away from you."

"So the blow-up?" I asked.

"Yup. And I nearly wrecked my phone when I threw it. Luckily it landed on the couch. And then I just overplayed it," said QB Earl.

"I thought it was real," said Sue. "I thought it triggered some episode."

"Me, too," said Lane. "I was scared."

"Good play, all of you," I said, "What was the story on the Wine Shop-pe?"

"Ha!" said Tom. "You wanted to go to the dive liquor store, but we had Judy at the Wine Shop-pe."

"I ran in ahead of you and saw Lido Bay was on sale right inside the door," said Lane.

"But you lied, saying only booze and beer," I said.

"And the wine was right in front of you, and you didn't even see it," said Sue, laughing. "The whole display in big letters."

"The place did smell awful and sour," I said.

"And NLP worked again!" said Lane.

"Good job," I said.

"Thanks to the Paraliminals," said Lane joyfully.

"What?"

"I was listening to the *New Behavior Generator* every day to make sure I could use the NLP techniques perfectly. And I was listening to *Belief* to build my internal belief that I could pull it off," said Lane.

"So that whole talk about you listening to the Paraliminals to get a new job was bunk?" I asked.

"I never said that," smiled Lane. "I said I had a big new goal, and I was using them for support. And I would not tell you the goal."

"I thought it was a new job."

"NLP works!" said Lane.

"Okay," I was smiling ear to ear. "But how come you didn't show up when we were canoeing?"

"I tried," said Judy.

"You tried?"

"I tried."

"We went downstream from where you were and launched the canoe, but Judy couldn't paddle upstream," said Paul.

"I tried," said Judy, laughing. "I tried."

"The harder she paddled the worse it got," said Paul. "She simply could not make headway. She tried zigzagging, but she still couldn't go fast enough."

"Plus, I was wearing out. Awfully fast. I had never been in a canoe, so I was starting at ground zero," she said.

"It was probably best," said QB Earl, "because seeing you probably would have upset Nels more."

"The way you were yanking me on," I said. "You kept me in a frenzy about Quarry Girl."

"I had to, otherwise you simply would have accepted her, that's who you are, and we wanted to keep you riled."

"Thanks guys. Much appreciated. But how the heck did you arrange the wedding?" I asked.

"That was the easiest of them all," said Paul.

"You see, we knew where the treasure was. We simply didn't know the route you would take. But we knew that the closer we got to the treasure, the easier it would be to set up experiences, such as the wedding."

"So that's why you had us go another forty-five miles further. To mesh with your grand scheme."

I felt like Hamlet. "I am but mad north-north-west. When the wind is southerly, I know a hawk from a handsaw."

26

Ball-peen Dings

JUDY AND I WERE SO DIFFERENT GROWING UP.

I had a litter of siblings, and she had herself.

I was so shy I would sit in a cubbyhole under the buffet when company would come over. Judy had her play tea set out serving play tea to everyone who walked through their back door.

In elementary school I could not aim at a kickball and actually kick it. The one time I did, I ran to third base instead of first, and any ball that came at me out in right field hit me and rolled away. Judy could jump rope in a double Dutch on one foot with eyes closed while spinning in circles reciting poetry.

In kindergarten I spent most of my days sitting behind the piano. In first grade I would pee my pants whenever the teacher called on me. In second grade the teacher made me stand in front of the class and then pointed out my wet spot. Another time I peed again when standing up front. She never called on me again.

Judy was fearless, outgoing, and no doubt had great bladder control.

I could do any math problem in my head, spell any word frontwards and backwards, and read twice as fast as anyone. As long as I could keep my mouth shut.

Judy stumbled with addition, spelling, and reading, but she could charm anyone into believing thirteen and fourteen equaled twenty-five, teeth was spelled with an *a*, and the story she just wove was the plot of the book.

In sixth grade I joined the Little League, but everyone on my team threatened to throw balls at me if I didn't quit. In seventh grade I joined basketball, and the coach was relieved when I sprained my ankle during the third practice session. In ninth grade the coach said, "You really shouldn't be out here." I just stood there looking at him, because I had no social interaction skills. He said, "All right, how about if you become the equipment manager," which I did, but when he asked me to throw him a basketball, I was never able to get it to move in the right direction. He said, "How about if you write about our games for the local weekly paper."

Well, that night I banged out a story on my Smith Corona Galaxie 12 typewriter and walked it to the publisher's house. He said, "Do you realize what time it is?" I just stood there looking at him.

He said, "All right, let me read it." Two minutes later, he said, "That's good kid, but you have to write about an actual game. You just can't make up games." I just stood there looking at him.

"All right, come back next week with a story about a real

game, and I'll pay you fifteen cents an inch."

I said, "Okay," and walked away knowing I would be back the next week.

He yelled out, "Hey kid, what's your name?"

I didn't hear him, because I was using my brainpower trying to figure out what "fifteen cents an inch" meant.

By the time I graduated from high school I was doing upwards of twenty stories a week on every goings on in the town, because I had figured out that I received fifteen cents for every column inch of articles in the paper (the paper's secretary had clued me in on it). I became the master of long headlines and intriguing subheads, which meant more column inches and more stacks of fifteen cents.

Landscape photos paid more than portraits, and to keep portraits from being cropped to a single column, all photos of individuals had fascinating backgrounds that warranted double columns. I was an entrepreneur, and writing was my business.

Once, the publisher looked at the paycheck before handing it to me, rolling his eyes, saying, "Well, here's some Popsicle money."

I simply looked at him, thought the idea of eye rolling was cool, took the check, and said to myself, "Popsicle money?! This is college money. I'm going to blow this pop shop." But, of course, I said nothing, because I needed more checks. Instead I went out and took a bunch of landscape photographs that he published the following week.

In high school I always received an A in the classroom. Judy always received an A on the sports field, in drama class, and with any instrument she picked up.

In woodworking shop class I started making a box for mom's knitting but ended up with a crooked box that could fit four decks of cards, if the decks had been slightly less wide. There were no shop classes in Judy's school, but in my school my best friend made an oak china cabinet for his mom. Judy could have done that.

Somewhere in my mid-twenties I developed coordination, and I became a darn good racquetball player, tennis player, anything I would do. Never was good at throwing a ball, though.

I learned to be outgoing, or less ingoing, as long as I had an easy chair in my closet for safety. And while I suffered through being social, people generally liked me. I may not have been the most exciting person anyone would know, but I did have a take on life slightly out of a parallel universe. Like the time I wrote a story about a priest buying billboards to get people to Mass on Sundays. I sold it to a half-dozen regional magazines around the country with a tweak here and a different quote there. One magazine wouldn't pay me. They said their advertisers weren't paying them. Still I called every week, until the editor said, "A hardware store is paying me in ball-peen hammers. Can I have him send them to you, and can we call it even?"

I said sure.

Then I called my dad to find out what a ball-peen hammer was.

Two weeks later three massively heavy boxes of ball-peen hammers arrived at my apartment, seventy-two in total. I gave one to anyone I knew wanted one. Most didn't. My dad took two; one for the garage and one for the house so he could show people what his boy Nels gave him.

I brought two cases to a hardware store down the street, told the guy my story and how I couldn't eat ball-peen hammers, and he offered to buy twelve of them from me at half wholesale. I was fine with that, because it paid more than the article would have paid—the editor apparently didn't know the value of a ball-peen hammer. But I told the hardware store guy I still had thirty-six hammers with me. What could I do with them? He said he didn't know, but acknowledged he found several cases of Baby Ben wind-up alarm clocks in his basement storage left over from a big promotion ten years earlier. He said he would trade me eighteen for eighteen of the hammers.

"What will I do with the alarm clocks?"

"They will make better Christmas gifts than ball-peen hammers."

With that I took home eighteen Baby Ben alarm clocks. I set them out on my dining room table and looked at them for days. They were all set to 10:10, which looked like smiley mouths. One night a little after ten, I wound them all up, and listened to them tick. I watched Johnny Carson, then off to bed I went.

Around six that next morning I heard a ringing from the dining room. What the heck was that, I thought. And then more ringing. More ringing. Those damn Baby Ben clocks were all preset to six, and they all began ringing. I ran out to turn them off before the neighbor began pounding on the walls. I couldn't grab them fast enough to push in the alarm buttons. As I knocked a bunch of them over, I spied the remaining ball-peen hammers in the corner. I paused, tempted to grab one and pound the bells out of the clocks, and that's when the neighbor began pounding on the wall, and when I had the brainstorm of the century.

That weekend I invited everyone to a New Year's Eve party under the theme, *Ringing in the New Year, Smashing out the Past*. At midnight, when eighteen Baby Ben alarm clocks began clanging from under sofa cushions, behind the TV, in the kitchen cabinets, behind books, and inside of wastepaper baskets, everyone simultaneously figured out why there was a tray of ball-peen hammers on the dining room table with festive ribbons tied below the brass heads. *The new year was ringing, and it was time to smash the past.*

I would find clock parts and ball-peen hammer dings in my apartment for months to come and, yes, I still had a stack of ball-peen hammers. But I had managed to pull off the most memorable New Year's party without relying solely on booze, while sharing the importance of letting go of the past. Smashing it if you need to.

Except for the few years when all of my friends were dying from AIDS, I guess I have had a pretty good life. Even those years were beautiful, because I learned to be present to what is important. Some of my friends turned militant. Others sunk into despair. Most rallied to figure out what to do and how to support each other. I marched on Washington, chanted nasty chants to President Reagan and the White House, protested the FDA, and paraded in New York City. I even wrote an opinion piece published in a major magazine:

> Thirty-four days after my friend Jeff was diagnosed with AIDS he died. Those were 34 gut-wrenching, yet incredibly touching and special days.

> Shortly after learning the diagnosis, Jeff asked me to run an errand. My mind raced. Was it safe to see him? Could I be in the same room? Could I hug him? Yes. Yes. Yes. I had heard that it's O.K. over and over, yet doubts crept in. Our conversation was awkward. I thought I had decided it was fine for me to be there. Yet I was tense. Then he asked, "Do you know what

it's like to tell your dad you're going to die?" My resistance fell. I hugged him with all the loving energy I could muster. From that moment on, I knew it was safe and right for me to be with Jeff.

In the next month, I witnessed a reuniting and bonding of a wonderful family that had been separated by many miles and misconceptions and the trials of day-to-day life. I saw an outpouring of compassion and unconditional love that I had never dreamed possible.

I also saw a disheartening side of human frailty in how some people reacted. A week after Jeff was diagnosed, I visited a friend. His kids jumped on me as usual. His wife yelled at me to stay away from the kids and at the kids to stay away from Uncle Nels. All because I had a friend with AIDS.

After Jeff died, the city daily published an article praising his life and accomplishments. The story identified me as a freelance writer and a close friend. People asked what I was going to do about the negative publicity. All because I had a friend die from AIDS.

These are just two examples of the images AIDS creates. Only education can eliminate them. This magazine is doing an exemplary job. But there is a piece missing: What do you do when someone you know has been diagnosed with the disease?

First, you forget about the need to know how the person was infected. The social stigma attached to the highest risk groups leads to judgments and gossip. No one has the right to pass judgment.

Only after you forget that need to know can you embrace my second suggestion, to turn on *unconditional love*. AIDS patients endure overpowering physical, emotional, and spiritual pain. They need all the unconditional love you can give.

Jeff had a caring family and strong friends. He died in a glow of sunshine and love. Not all AIDS patients are as blessed.

As you can imagine, back in 1987 that piece generated mailbags of letters, just as emotional as Jeff's final days. Most were supportive, many had sad stories, and a few were hateful. But in all of it I realized the ability we all have to make a difference in the lives of others. Yes, I fully believe our purpose on this planet is to live a life of happiness and joy, and I believe we can all help others experience this themselves.

Enough about me and my once cause célèbre, because someone fresh has my spirit. Judy. We'll start a new chapter for her.

27

In Our Nature

I LOVE THE SURREAL.

The treasure hunt was certainly surreal. Everything from the League of Uncommon Gentlemen to the Butterscotch Clipper to the wedding. Everything in between and within. Judy Marie. I still can't wrap my head around it. And maybe for you surreal is trying to solve the treasure hunt of this book. Where the heck is it?

Don't worry. You can spend a lot of time figuring out the clues and find it, which would be super cool. I'll open a bottle of champagne with you. Or, like me and the treasure hunt that Lane, Judy, QB Earl, Tom, and Paul created, perhaps it will just come together for you. I suspect that the person who finds the treasure will be someone reading this book and thinking, "OMG, I get it. I know where it is!"

That's part of Judy's story. At least after college.

She made it through a liberal arts college like me, not really knowing what she would be doing. I knew that writing would be part of my life, but was not sure how. She knew she had gifts of charm and getting people to love her and listen to her, and somehow that would play into her life.

After college she met Bryan, who was two days younger than she. He was the type of guy that everyone would fall in love with. Straight women and gay men. Same with Lane, but with Lane it was his Persian blues that hypnotized people. Bryan, on the other hand, simply had good looks. Longish black wavy hair. Full lips. Welcoming eyes. And a warm personality that oozed compassion. He was genuinely interested in other human beings. Everyone loved that about him. And when he smiled, everything on the planet was all right.

And it was for Judy.

Within two years they were married, and a year later he lay dead in a coffin at the front of his childhood church, with a peaceful look on his face that said everything was good and all was right.

Although it licked him physically, the rare and odd disease that infiltrated his body was no match for his personality. Even until the final breath, everyone believed a miracle would blossom, he would sit up, and they would have a pizza party.

In those final moments of his life, when he drifted in and out of consciousness, Judy saw a beautiful golden glow in the upper corner of the hospital room. It was warm, comforting, and awe inspiring. She suspected it was his guardian angel and wondered whether others would see it. She was alone with Bryan in suspended time. As he took that final breath, the golden glow embraced the entire room. Every cell in her body was soothed, bathed in the golden light. Bryan was at peace. Still,

Judy sank into a three-year funk, further fueled by her divorcing parents, believing her soul mate had been sucked from her life, like her birth father (me), like everything good that would come her way long into the future.

In the depths she would have ended her life had she not found the idea of suicide so repulsive, thinking she was put here to suffer, to wear Queen Victoria-black until she herself passed on.

My rib cage crushed in when Judy told the story. Lane cried. Sue cried. QB Earl sat there. Tom bowed his head. How could someone so sweet and exceedingly special suffer so much.

"Until one day I was walking through a park," she told us. "I felt like someone was talking to me. I didn't hear a voice, yet someone was talking to me. Someone I loved. But it wasn't Bryan. It wasn't my mom. It was different from that. I looked up, and it was as if the clouds in the sky were speaking. But without words. All of the clouds simultaneously. I knew what they were saying. For the first time, I finally understood everything. Why I was here. Who Bryan was. The planet, the trees, the grass, the birds, the dogs in the distance. I felt at peace. Thoroughly contented for having known Bryan. I looked around and kept repeating silently, 'I got it. I got it.' Everything changed, but nothing changed. It was as if it were there all along, waiting for me to discover it."

I'm not sure I understood all that Judy said. No one did. Lane commented, "That's beautiful. What were you experiencing? I want that." It was almost a *When Harry Met Sally* moment had we not been totally absorbed in her story.

"I later learned I had had a spiritual awakening," said Judy. We all just sat there.

"I know it sounds weird, but it was the most beautiful and

natural and sense-making experience of my life. Like I said, I finally got it. And for the next few weeks I went through life knowing the explanation to everything. Everything from personal interactions to politics to why the clerk at the store was the way he was to how the dogs and I were connected to boulders and trees. The moon and stars."

Judy said from that day forward she ceased worrying about anything. Even Bryan. She knew he was okay, and that the experience for her was just fine. She no longer suffered his loss. The clouds of the funk dissipated like the morning mist burned off by the rising sun. She became once again engaged in the world, happy to be alive, as expansive as she was before Bryan's death, and ready for someone new to come into her life.

Within a couple of months Judy accepted a position with a private investment company, which shocked the daylights out of everyone in her life. She had no aptitude in math, finance, or anything remotely detail-oriented. But one night she dreamed of changing the world by investing in opportunities for—changing the world.

Her title was Balance Specialist. No one in the company knew what Judy did all day. Neither did the partners, except for the partner who hired her, the one who dreamed of changing the world by investing in opportunities for—yes, changing the world.

They both had the same vision, and he felt Judy would be worth the sixty thousand dollars a year risk to seeing his vision through, even if it meant he needed to reduce his own compensation to appease the partners. But since they all took home nearly a million each, they agreed to follow his hunch.

Judy wasn't looking for that kind of job, although she would have been the first to say she was underemployed at the time, not meeting any potential. And he wasn't looking for a person like her, but they had a Reese's Peanut Butter Cup moment on a street corner. They connected immediately and began talking like two people drawn into love (or at least infatuation). Their bodies weren't tingling, but they were vibrating in a rare connection of vision, mission, and purpose.

At her new job Judy couldn't read the company reports, because they meant nothing to her. "Worse than Greek," she told her friends. But she sat in meeting after meeting just watching the interactions and flow of data. She met with the financial analysts, most of whom were her age but thirty or forty times more knowledgeable. In hearing how they talked about investment opportunities, she knew whether the businesses were good for the world and, as a side benefit, good for the company. It was all a game for her, and one she played well.

Within three years Judy was making almost two hundred thousand a year, all because she was holding to a vision she shared with her boss. She seemed to have unique insights into every opportunity that presented itself. It's not that they acted on all of Judy's recommendations, but those they did hit pay dirt for their company and for the world.

Everything she said fit with everything I learned from the *Seeds of Enlightenment* course, which I have mentioned a couple of times in this book (hint, hint). Jeddah's teachings had given me glimpses into the world Judy lives every day.

Lane asked Judy, "Does this mean you are enlightened?"

QB Earl was nonplussed by the question. Sue's rubies vibrated. Tom just waited for the answer.

"I don't know," she said. "I began googling a lot to see what had happened to me, and it seemed that the phrase 'spiritual awakening' fit. So did 'enlightenment,' at least to a certain extent. Everyone seems to think enlightenment is something special, but it really isn't. It is seeing the world—the universe—the way it is. It's when we stop fooling ourselves. It's the mist lifting. It's not like I ascended or attained something. It was more like I walked through a door into another room where the drama and suffering of life was absent."

Like I said, everything in Judy's experience fit with everything I knew, but I suspected the difference was that she knew beyond the shadow of the doubt, whereas I knew intellectually, not from complete experience. Judy just lives it. I have to live it as a value in my life, constantly checking a checklist of dos and don'ts. It's like the difference between someone who could naturally throw a baseball and someone who has practiced to the point where they can throw (neither of which I can do, by the way, although I am wicked on the racquetball court). It's like someone who can sing with perfect pitch and someone who needs to be conscious about it (again, I can't sing, but I can play a wicked album).

I loved hearing all of Judy's stories and looking at the pictures on her iPad, especially how she landed in Bali and met Tom. "I could bloody well afford to stay at most any place on the island, but I was traveling with one of my less financially endowed friends. And while I could have treated her to a room, she's the type for whom that would not sit well, so I stayed in a place she could afford and played my flute outside the resort Tom stayed, where I really wanted to stay. Oh well. I guess one way or another, the universe was going to bring us together."

It was hard for me not to think of the two hundred thousand dollar fund I had been building for Judy, and how it was probably just a drop in her money bucket, but someday I'll give it to her, and what she does with it is totally up to her.

She could give it away, I suppose, but I'm thinking she'll more likely invest in one of the funds of the company she works for. They apparently make good returns for their investors, and she knows how to get them into investments that make a difference. Granted, their firm has invested over forty billion through the years, but her energy must be doing something good for the company.

All my life all I did was hope Judy was happy. I'm saddened I wasn't there for her dark years, and I am delighted beyond delighted how she lives on purpose a happy and joyous life. Some of us need to work at it, but for her it's completely second nature. Or, should I say, it is in her nature. It is in all of ours, but we seem to put a lot of crap in the way of it.

Lane's really onto something by listening to those Paraliminals, because they are doing the next best thing to a spiritual awakening. They are cleaning up his emotions and issues and helping him live a great life. When we talked about them, Judy said, "I'm thinking Paraliminals would be good for me, too. I certainly have issues with procrastination and a bad habit here and there."

Don't we all.

28

Sudden Illumination of Joy

A FEW DAYS AFTER WE RETURNED from the treasure hunt, Tom's dedication party for the Frogyrinth was upon us. Frog Day.

We gathered early in the day to help Tom and Paul prepare the feast. We were expecting fifty to sixty people, maybe more since we made sure more of my friends and Judy's friends would be there. Yes, we were unveiling the Frogyrinth, but we were also unveiling each other. We had been keeping it a secret those few days, so no one had any inkling of what was to come. Heck, very few of my friends even knew I had a daughter. At first I didn't want anyone to know. I didn't want anyone talking me into keeping the kid. Then it became such a huge void in my life that I didn't want anyone to be sucked into my emptiness.

During Frog Day we would fly the last two frogs, dedicate

the Frogyrinth, walk the Frogyrinth, partake in a feast, and enjoy a special concert by Judy.

You may remember, each of the frogs had to sit on concrete pedestals, in part to give them height and in part to keep them off the wet ground. But how the heck do you lift 880-pound limestone frogs?

You don't.

You fly them!

Tom has a Ditch Witch skid steer. It's a piece of construction equipment he uses for doing projects on the property. He purchased it after the banishment when he could no longer borrow Fred's Bobcat. It has various attachments including forks so he can lift pallets, boulders, and frogs.

All but two of the frogs had been flown before the treasure hunt. We saved two for Frog Day, because everyone wanted to see how it was done.

Tom used the forks to haul each fat and happy frog on its pallet to the Frogyrinth. The rest of us followed along in the first-ever Frog Parade. For each frog, he lifted the pallet onto the concrete pedestal. He backed up the forks, raised them, and moved forward so the forks were about two feet above the head of the frog.

We took a bright yellow tow strap and wrapped it around the frog's waist. On the left side of its waist, we threaded a red tow strap through the yellow strap. We brought up the two ends of the red strap to hook on one of the forks above, spreading the hooks for stability. We used another red tow strap to do the same on the right side of the frog. And finally we strapped a blue tow strap to the yellow strap on the frog's butt, over his head, through the red straps, up to the frame of the forks. This would balance the frog, keeping him from swinging backwards.

QB Earl used a reciprocating saw to cut away the supports coming up from the pallets. The pallets were originally the crates that held the frogs during their trip from Bali. Tom and Paul had already removed the top of the crates, because they had appeared to pen in the frogs. "I swear they began singing as soon as we removed the top part of the crates," Tom said. Paul would smile and nod.

When the frog was free from the pallet, Tom gently lifted the frog attached to the forks by the four straps. We pulled out the pallet and forcibly swung the frog to center her on the concrete pedestal.

When we flew the first frog a few weeks earlier we had only one strap, which proved nearly catastrophic. The center of gravity of the frog shifted as soon as Tom raised the forks. We thought it would flip backwards and crack, but we manhandled it. And ninety minutes later we had the frog beautifully sitting on the pedestal.

These last two frogs on Frog day took only five minutes each. We had become professional frog fliers, a profession without much call. But if anyone needs to fly frogs, we will do it quickly and effortlessly.

While those gathered expected something a little more harrowing, they enjoyed the choreography of our flying frogs, and our swift success meant we could open the wine sooner. The rules had been clearly posted: *No booze will be served until after the day's flying. No children under 48 inches allowed within 20 yards of the flying equipment.*

It was time for the dedication ceremony.

"Since moving here I've fantasized building a labyrinth," said Tom. Everyone gathered closely to listen. Judy's friend filming as he had during the treasure hunt.

"When in Bali, a year ago December, we were greeted by fat and happy frogs playing Balinese musical instruments on the property we were staying. They had been carved fifty years earlier out of gray lava, coming to life playing the enchanting music of Bali. That's the music you hear coming from the Frogyrinth right now.

"During the eighth night I dreamt of the frogs coming back with us and finding their home in a labyrinth, which they called a Frogyrinth. I sketched the Frogyrinth, showing it to my friends at breakfast, and within hours we were in the van scouring the island for fat and happy frogs.

"Two nights later two friends who live on Bali joined us for dinner. We told them of the frogs and the Frogyrinth, and all I remember from the evening was Renate saying, 'I know a carver. Let's get him to carve the frogs for you.'

"Five months later the white limestone frogs were on the ocean floating here.

"The Frogyrinth is a labyrinth. A labyrinth is not a maze. You can get lost in a maze, but you cannot get lost in a labyrinth. It has only one path, and once we choose to enter it, we make a magnificent choice. It is like our journey through life. In a labyrinth it is impossible to get lost.

"As we stand here at its entrance, we can see its center. It's the frog sitting in the lotus position, Renate. Each frog is named after our friends on our adventure. This first frog here is Ketut. He was our driver who took care of us. And then we have Karyn, Robert, my partner Paul, Joe, Bobbi, me, and Renate. I'll take you around and introduce you to the frogs in their stations in a bit.

"As I was saying, you can see the center, but in ten years the bushes between the paths will be six to twelve feet tall. You will not be able to see the destination, but it is a labyrinth, and in a labyrinth there is only one way to walk. You cannot get lost. While you may not always see what is in front of you, you will always get to your center, and when you are ready you can always walk back to the beginning. It's a great metaphor for life.

"Historically a labyrinth is an ancient mystical tool. Use it to take a meaningful journey...to the center...to the center of you.

"There are many ways to walk the Frogyrinth. There is no right way or wrong way. You can only succeed. Some will walk in quiet contemplation. Others in prayer. Some will walk with a life goal in mind. And some will simply walk with friends... and wine.

"The Frogyrinth is for the sudden illumination of joy. The charms are already in place. There is nothing you need do other than walk, greet the fat and happy frogs, and absorb their joy. As you walk into the center, feel complete and utter happiness, knowing everything you want in life will unfold for you.

"The Frogyrinth mysteriously began working eighteen months ago in Bali, before the frogs were even carved. Early one morning I heard the beautiful sound of a bamboo flute on the beach in front of our place." Tom gazed over to Judy and smiled.

"I spoke with the young flutist and found she lived just down the road from here. I told her about the frogs and invited her to this dedication party. She was eager to come. She offered to bring her flute, and, of course, I accepted. I'm happy to say that after dinner, she'll perform for us the same captivating sounds from Bali." Folks applauded.

"There's something else we'd like to share with you." Tom

paused. "Judy, will you come here for me?" Judy walked up. Everyone was happy—wine, sun, friends, and all—and I struggled with silent gasps of emotion, about to break into tears. Judy was so beautiful, wearing the same wispy lace from the pretend wedding and a crown of wildflowers picked in the woods around Tom's place. Tom put his arm around Judy. She leaned into him, smiling, so happy. He smelled her flowers.

"As I said, the Frogyrinth began spinning its magic eighteen months ago in Bali, bringing Judy to me, to you today. And why is that so special? Because of a big secret. Something we discovered just a few months ago, hidden away for thirty years, not by the choice of anyone here, but by the choice of others wanting to control a situation, perhaps well intentioned, but it kept hearts away. Hearts that were meant to be together." Tom spoke slowly and deliberately. "Now is the time for the frogs to release a sudden illumination of joy."

He looked in everyone's eyes.

"Judy is the long-lost daughter of my best friend, Nels."

What?! Nels has a daughter?! Nels? What? Daughter!

I lost it then. Those exclamations registered only as murmurs as I walked toward Judy—my golden ring, with my arms wide open.

Everyone quieted, bathed in purple rain and a sudden illumination of joy. Wine glasses cheered into the air as our friends closed around us, cocooning us, birds singing, and the sun glistening on the Butterscotch Clipper off in the distance. Tom had purchased it after all.